INTRODUCTION TO DECLARER'S PLAY

EDWIN B. KANTAR

WILSHIRE BOOK COMPANY
9731 VARIEL AVENUE
CHATSWORTH, CALIFORNIA 91311

Introduction to Declarer's Play
by Edwin B. Kantar

© 1968 by Prentice-Hall, Inc.

Copyright under International and Pan American
Copyright Conventions

Library of Congress Catalog Card Number: 67-25627

Printed in the United States of America

ISBN 0-87980-401-7

Prentice-Hall International, Inc., *London*
Prentice-Hall of Australia, Pty. Ltd., *Sydney*
Prentice-Hall of Canada, Ltd., *Toronto*
Prentice-Hall of India Private Ltd., *New Delhi*
Prentice-Hall of Japan, Inc., *Tokyo*

Contents

Part I—Notrump Play

1.	Sure Tricks	3
2.	Establishing Tricks	9
3.	Taking Tricks with the Spot-Cards	17
4.	Taking Tricks by Finessing	24
5.	The Hold-Up Play	39
6.	The Danger Hand	59

Part II—Trump Play

7.	The Trump Suit	73
8.	Counting Losers	77
9.	Creating Extra Winners	91
10.	Long Suit Establishment	113
11.	Trumping in the Short Hand	131
	Index	145

Part I

NOTRUMP PLAY

♠ ♡ ◇ ♣

1

Sure Tricks

♠   ♡   ◇   ♣

The game of bridge revolves around the bidding for and the taking of tricks. In this book we are not worried about the bidding—just the taking.

The most important single move that you must make before playing out a hand is to count your tricks. That seems easy enough, doesn't it?

Let's take a simple example:

DUMMY
♠ A 4 3

YOU
♠ K 5 2

Whenever you play a bridge hand, you get to see all of your partner's cards before you play. Your partner's hand is called the dummy—and that term has nothing to do with the way he may have bid his hand.

So what you do after the opponent on your left makes an opening lead is to look at one suit at a time; look, for example, at your spades and at dummy's spades and count the number of sure tricks you have in that suit. Then you go through the same process in each suit and come up with a figure. That is a very important figure. It tells you how many tricks you can take at a moment's notice. Remember that term—*sure tricks*—because we are going to work with it for a while.

Now let's go back to our example. In dummy we have the A 4 3 of spades, and in our own hand we have the K 5 2.

The ace will take one trick and the king will take another, so we have the two sure spade tricks. This may seem elementary, but you will never learn to play a hand unless you do this.

Counting tricks has its hazards. Let's try this one:

DUMMY
♠ K Q

YOU
♠ A 2

Now how many sure tricks do you have in spades? This answer is two, not three. You see, when you play a card from your hand, you must also take a card from the dummy. Let's say you play the ace; then the queen must be played from dummy. That leaves you with the two in your hand and the king in dummy. In other words, you have two tricks, not three.

The important thing to see is that you can never take more tricks in a suit than there are cards in the longer of the two hands. Look:

DUMMY
♠ A K Q

YOU
♠ J 10

Between you and your dummy you have the ace, king, queen, jack, and ten. But you can only take three tricks. That is because the dummy, which is the longer hand in spades, has only three cards.

Practice counting sure tricks with these examples:

(a) DUMMY
     ♠ K Q 3

     YOU
     ♠ A 5 2

(b) DUMMY
     ♠ A Q J 8

     YOU
     ♠ K 7

(c) DUMMY
♠ A J 3

YOU
♠ K Q 5 4

(d) DUMMY
♠ Q J 10 5 4

YOU
♠ A K 3

Solutions

(a) Three tricks. You can take them in any order you like. You could play the king, then the queen, and then the three to your ace; or you could play the ace, and then a little one to the king, and then the queen. Or you could play the king, then the three to your ace, and then a little one back to your queen. You see, when you have an even number of cards in both hands (e.g., three cards on each side), you have quite a bit of flexibility. You would have to see all 26 cards before you knew which hand you wanted to end up in. I am merely showing you that you don't always have to play the ace first when taking tricks.

(b) Four tricks. Now this situation and the following ones are a little different because you do not have an even number of cards on both sides. In this case the dummy has four and you only have two. As a general rule, whenever you have a bunch of good tricks in a suit that is unevenly divided, *you should play the high card(s) from the short side first.* This means playing the king, which will take the eight from dummy, and then leading your seven over to the ace, queen, and jack in dummy. When cards are high it does not matter which one you play first. In this case, when you have played the king and are about to lead the seven over to the dummy, it doesn't matter if you play the jack, queen, or ace—they are all the same. In this little game we are playing, we are always assuming that the opponents have led some other suit and we have taken the trick. Now we are about to play our suit. Sometimes the trick we have taken will have been in dummy. Therefore, if the lead is in the dummy, we must play the eight of spades over to our king and then the seven back to the dummy. But in either case we are playing the high card from the short side first.

(c)   Four tricks. If the lead is in the dummy (from the prior play), we should first play the ace, then the jack, and then the three over to our king and queen. Notice that we played the high cards from the short side first. Things would be exactly the same if the lead were in our hand. We would play the four over to the ace (or jack), then the jack, and then the three over to our king and queen. It is conceivable that the opponents might lead this suit themselves, in which case we would still play it the same way.

(d)   Five tricks. This time we would play the king and ace (or the ace and king) from our hand and then lead the three over to the queen, jack, and ten in the dummy.

Playing the high card or high cards from the short side first allows us to end up on the long side, where we can take the maximum amount of tricks.

Now let's practice counting our sure tricks in an entire hand:

DUMMY
♠ A 4 3
♡ K 4
♢ 10 8 7 5
♣ A K Q 3

YOU
♠ 7 5 2
♡ A Q 3
♢ A 4 3 2
♣ J 4 2

Let's pretend the final contract was 3 NT and West, your left-hand opponent, led the king of spades. How many sure tricks do you have in the *entire* hand?

You should have come up with nine sure tricks. You have one in spades, three in hearts, one in diamonds, and four in clubs.

Sometimes counting tricks and taking them are two different things. But if you remember about the high card from the short hand, you will not have any trouble. In clubs, you would play the jack first from your own hand and then play a little one over to the ace, king, and queen in dummy. In hearts, you would play the king first and then the four over to the ace and queen in your own hand.

Here are a couple more practice hands. Count your sure tricks and see what you come up with:

(a)	DUMMY	(b)	DUMMY
	♠ K Q 3		♠ K Q J
	♡ A J		♡ Q J 10 9
	◇ A J 7 6		◇ J 10 9
	♣ K 4 3 2		♣ K Q J
	YOU		YOU
	♠ A 4		♠ 10 9 8
	♡ K Q		♡ K 8 7 6
	◇ K Q 8 3 2		◇ K Q 8 7
	♣ A 7 6 5		♣ 10 9

Solutions

(a) You should have come up with twelve tricks: three in spades, two in hearts (make sure you see why), five in diamonds (playing the ace and jack first), and two in clubs.

(b) You have zero sure tricks! That's right, not one. In order to take tricks in any one of these suits, you must first get rid of the opponent's ace. Until you get rid of that ace, you do not have a sure trick. The definition of a sure trick is a trick which you can take *without giving up the lead*. When you must give up the lead to take a trick, you are *establishing tricks*, which leads us to the next chapter.

KEY POINTERS

(1)   The first step in playing a bridge hand is to count your *sure tricks*.

(2)   A sure trick is a trick which can be taken without giving up the lead.

(3)   You can never take more tricks in a suit than there are cards in the longer hand. (If both you and your dummy have two cards in one suit, the most tricks you can take in that suit is two.)

(4)   When taking sure tricks, play the high cards(s) from the short side first. This will allow you to end up on the long side, where you can cash the rest of the tricks in the suit.

2

Establishing Tricks

♠   ♡   ◇   ♣

In most of the hands that you play, you never seem to have enough sure tricks to make your contract. Let's say you are playing 3 NT. You need nine tricks to fulfill your contract, and you usually count up only five or six sure tricks. What are you going to do? Well, there is another method of getting tricks—but it involves a little work. You have to *establish*, or make, tricks for yourself. Study this diagram:

DUMMY
♠ K Q J

YOU
♠ 4 3 2

If this is your spade suit, you do not have a sure trick in spades. But if you were to play the king (or the queen or jack) from dummy and drive out the ace, you could establish two spade tricks for yourself. This method of establishing tricks—driving out the opponent's aces and kings—is the most common method of obtaining tricks in bridge.

You may be wondering what would happen if the opponents did not take their ace—actually it would turn out the same. Let's say you lead the king and everyone plays low. Well, you've taken one trick already. Now you lead the queen. If everyone plays low again, you have taken two tricks in the suit, and that is all you ever had coming in the first place.

When it comes to establishing tricks, you follow the same

general rule that you did when you were taking your sure tricks. Play the high card(s) from the short side. For example:

DUMMY
♠ Q J 10 3

YOU
♠ K 2

Let's say you wish to establish some spade tricks for yourself. You should lead the king from your own hand. If the opponent takes it with the ace, you will still have the deuce, and the next time it is your lead you can take the queen, jack, and ten. In other words, you should get three tricks from this suit.

Now let's practice counting tricks in suits that we must establish. How many tricks can you establish in each of the following suits, and which card do you play first?

(a)   DUMMY   (b)   DUMMY
      ♠ K Q 7   ♠ Q 5
      YOU   YOU
      ♠ J 3   ♠ K J 10 9 3

(c)   DUMMY   (d)   DUMMY
      ♠ 4 3 2   ♠ A 3
      YOU   YOU
      ♠ Q J 10   ♠ Q J 10 9

Solutions

(a)   Two tricks. You should play the jack first. If the lead is in the North hand, lead the seven to the jack.

(b)   Four tricks. You should play the queen first. If the lead is in the South hand, you should lead the three to the queen.

(c)   One trick. You can lead this from either hand because you have an even number of cards on both sides. The queen will drive out the king, the jack will drive out the ace, and the ten will be an established trick.

(d)   Three tricks. You should lead the ace and then the three. If you live right, the king might fall under the ace, and then you will get four tricks—but don't count on it. They have too many cards in the suit.

You are now ready to make a little progress. Your next step is to count the sure tricks you have and see how many more tricks you can establish.

The important thing to remember is to keep the two counts separate *until you have actually established some tricks*. Once you establish some tricks, you can add the tricks you have established to your sure trick count.

Take a look at this hand:

DUMMY
♠ A 4 3
♡ K Q J 10
♢ K 5 2
♣ 9 8 7

YOU
♠ K 5
♡ 5 4 3 2
♢ A Q J 9
♣ A K Q

Let's say you are playing a contract of 6 NT. You must always ask yourself how many tricks you need to make your contract. In this case you need twelve (six plus your bid). The opponents lead the queen of spades. Now after realizing how many tricks you need, which is really the first step, you must add up your sure tricks. So let's do that. You have two in spades, four in diamonds, and three in clubs. A total of nine. Notice that you did not count even one sure trick in hearts, simply because you cannot take a trick in that suit until you drive out the ace.

Well, you have nine sure tricks and you must establish at

least three more tricks in hearts to make your contract. That's easy enough. You simply win the spade with your king and lead a heart. Let's assume that the opponents take it with their ace. Your sure trick count has just changed. You now have twelve sure tricks instead of nine, because you can add those extra three heart tricks to your total once the ace has been removed.

Now for the most important point in the whole lesson. *When playing a bridge hand that does not have enough sure tricks, you must establish extra tricks. Establishing extra tricks is the first thing you do. You establish extra tricks before you take your sure tricks. Then, when you have established enough tricks to make your contract, you take all of your tricks at once.*

Rules are no good unless you know the reason. So we are going to go back to our 6 NT hand. For the first time we are going to look at all four hands.

DUMMY
♠ A 4 3
♡ K Q J 10
◇ K 5 2
♣ 9 8 7

WEST
♠ Q J 10
♡ A
◇ 10 8 7 6 4
♣ J 4 3 2

EAST
♠ 9 8 7 6 2
♡ 9 8 7 6
◇ 3
♣ 10 6 5

YOU
♠ K 5
♡ 5 4 3 2
◇ A Q J 9
♣ A K Q

For the time being don't worry about why West led the queen of spades. In just a short time you will see why. Presently you are worried about taking twelve tricks.

Notice that after you take the first trick with the king of spades, you still have control (that is, you can take the next trick) in all suits except hearts, where you will soon be establishing your tricks.

What if you were to take your club tricks before knocking out the ace of hearts? Watch closely what would happen so that you never make this error—in fact, the most common error beginners make—of taking their sure tricks too quickly.

If you were to take your three club tricks before playing hearts, West would still have the jack of clubs. It would be the only club left. Then, when you led a heart, West would take it with his ace and then would be able to take the next trick with his jack of clubs because you had surrendered control of the club suit by taking your sure tricks too quickly.

The same thing would happen in diamonds. If, after winning the first trick with the king of spades, you were to take four tricks in diamonds, West would still have one diamond. Then, when you played a heart, West would take that trick with the ace of hearts and the next trick with the ten of diamonds. In neither case would you make your contract, because you would have lost two tricks, while you can afford to lose only one in a contract of six.

Therefore, it is important that you see that by taking your sure tricks too quickly, you give up control in the suit, and—even worse—you establish tricks for your opponents!

Establish first: Take your sure tricks after you have established.

Now you are going to practice counting your sure tricks, seeing if you have tricks that can be established (and, if so, how many), and finally, determining which suit you should play first.

(a)

DUMMY
♠ K Q 10 3
♡ A 4 3
♢ 7 6 5
♣ K Q 2

YOU
♠ J 5
♡ K 5 2
♢ A 8 4 3
♣ A J 10 9

Contract: 3 NT
Lead: Queen of hearts

(b)   DUMMY
                       ♠ A K 5
                       ♡ 3 2
                       ◇ A 7 6 5
                       ♣ 5 4 3 2

                       YOU
                       ♠ Q 7
                       ♡ Q J 10 9
                       ◇ K 4 3 2
                       ♣ A K 6

Contract: 3 NT
Lead: Jack of spades

(a)   How many sure tricks do you count?
(b)   How many more can you establish?
(c)   Which suit should you play first?
(d)   Which card should you play in that suit?

Solutions

(a)   You have seven sure tricks and you can establish
      three more in spades. You should play spades first
      (after taking the first trick with the king of hearts)
      and you should lead the jack. If it takes the trick, you
      continue with spades until one of your opponents
      plays the ace. You will eventually wind up with ten
      tricks. Once you have driven out the ace of spades,
      you will have established enough tricks to make your
      contract. Then you can take all of your tricks at once.
(b)   You have seven sure tricks and you can establish two
      more in hearts. Therefore, you should play hearts
      first. After taking the first trick in your hand (high
      card from short side), you can begin by playing any
      heart (although declarer usually plays his highest
      equal, or highest in a sequence, first, which is the

way it will be done in this book). So you would first lead the queen of hearts. In this case you must give up the lead twice in hearts in order to establish two tricks of your own in the suit. Assume that the queen loses to the king or ace and that a spade is returned. You take this in the dummy and lead another heart, establishing your hearts before taking any of your sure tricks.

KEY POINTERS

(1)   When playing a hand, know how many tricks you must take to fulfill your contract.

(2)   Count your sure tricks and if you do not have enough, look for suits which can be *established*—usually suits which are missing the ace or the king. Once you lose a trick to the high card, the rest of your cards in that suit will be good.

(3)   Do your establishing early. Establish first and then take your sure tricks.

(4)   If you take your sure tricks too soon, you will find that when you start establishing, the opponents will by that time have good tricks established in the suits in which you hastily cashed your sure tricks.

(5)   Don't be afraid to give up the lead. On most hands you must give up the lead two or three times.

(6)   When playing equal cards (such as the jack, ten, and nine), declarer should usually play his highest equal first. This applies to both establishing and taking. By doing this, you make it harder for the opponents to know what is going on. If you have the ace, king, and queen of spades and you play the queen, naturally it will take the trick, but your opponents will know that you still have the king and ace. However, if you play the ace first, the opponents will not know who has the king and queen.

When playing equal cards from the dummy, it doesn't matter which one you play first, because the opponents can see the dummy. However, just to stay in practice, you should take the highest equal from dummy also.

3

Taking Tricks with the Spot-Cards

♠ ♡ ◇ ♣

Until this chapter you have been overwhelming your opponents with aces and kings. Either you have had enough sure tricks to make your contract, or you could establish your kings and queens by driving out an ace or perhaps an ace and a king. Unfortunately, life doesn't always run so smoothly. You must learn how to win tricks with your deuces and threes as well as with the more regal members of the deck.

The first and most important point to be made in this chapter is the value of length. Once you can appreciate this, your bidding will improve appreciably.

Let's start with a simple example:

DUMMY

♠ 6 5 4

WEST   EAST

♠ 8 7 3   ♠ J 10 9

YOU

♠ A K Q 2

Let's say you are playing this suit in notrump. You play the ace, king, and queen, and your opponents follow to all three rounds. Since twelve spades have been played, your deuce is the last spade and is, therefore, a good trick. In this case you are very lucky that each of your opponents held three spades. Had one of them started with four spades, your deuce would not have been good.

But how do you know whether your deuce is good or not? You would have to have counted. Each time a spade was led and everyone followed, you would see four spades played. Three times four is twelve, so your deuce is the only one left.

Maybe you can see another problem with this type of suit. How many *sure tricks* should you count for the A K Q 2 facing the 6 5 4? You should count three sure tricks, but you should make a mental note that the fourth spade *might* be good if the opponents spades are divided 3-3.

How often will the fourth card in a suit take a trick? Look at this example:

DUMMY
♠ 7 5

YOU
♠ A K Q 2

Can you count on a possible trick from your two of spades? No. This time you only have six spades between your hand and dummy, leaving the opponents with the remaining seven. If their spades are divided as evenly as possible (that is, one hand having four and the other three), your two of spades will not be good— unless perhaps the hand with the four spades makes a mistake and throws one away early in the play.

Eventually you will see that if you and your partner have seven or more cards in any one suit between the two hands, there is *always* a chance to make at least one extra trick.

Here is an extreme case in point:

DUMMY
♠ 6 5 4

WEST   **EAST**
♠ A Q J   ♠ K 10 9

YOU
♠ 8 7 3 2

(Incidentally, you should be laying these cards out in front of you as we go along, in order to see things more clearly.)

Here you have the seven smallest cards between your hand and dummy. Yet, if you absolutely had to establish one trick in this suit, you could so. However, you must have patience and a little luck.

What you would have to do is play the suit three times. Each time you led the suit, their big cards would fall on each other. In the end, after you had played the suit three times, your fourth card would be good because it would be the only spade in play.

Another way to look at this is to pretend that you are West. If you were taking tricks in spades and East was the dummy, you could only take three tricks. (Remember, you can never take more tricks than there are cards in the longer of the two hands.) And after you took your three tricks, South would wind up with the last spade.

Let's hope that you never are so desperate that you must establish a suit where you are missing the A K Q J 10 9! But it can be done.

Before we discuss five- and six-card suits, let's take a look at another familiar face:

DUMMY

♠ 5 4 3

WEST   EAST

♠ A 10 9   ♠ 8 7 6

YOU

♠ K Q J 2

The moment you see the K Q J together, you should be thinking about driving out the ace in order to make at least two tricks. But now you can become a little more greedy. Since you have seven cards between the two hands, you might be able to establish your little one as well.

In this case you could lead the king (or lead towards the king from the North hand) and drive out the ace. Your queen and jack would then be good, and if everyone followed suit, your little deuce would be a trick also. Whatever happens, don't scorn your low cards if they are attached to long suits. Learn to appreciate those little guys—they are worth their weight in gold.

Now that you have seen the value of a total of seven cards between your hand and the dummy, just think of all the fun you will have when you have eight or nine cards in the same suit!

Let's talk about eight cards between your hand and the dummy. These eight cards are most likely to be divided 4-4, 5-3, or 6-2 between the two hands. In the opponents' hands, the remaining five cards will usually be divided 3-2 and occasionally 4-1.

Let's start with a simple one:

DUMMY

♠ 5 4 3 2

WEST   EAST

♠ Q J 9   ♠ 10 8

YOU

♠ A K 7 6

Here you could play your ace and king, which would leave only one spade in the opponents' hands. You could then give them their trick, but in turn you would establish your fourth spade and dummy's fourth spade as well. But remember, you can only take one extra trick with that fourth spade, because your spade and dummy's will fall together on the same trick.

What should you think before you start playing a suit like this? You should think: I have eight spades between my hand and dummy, leaving the opponents with five spades. If their five spades are divided 3-2 (which is the most likely distribution), I can establish my fourth spade by playing the suit three times and exhausting the spades of both opponents.

It is important to see that you must lose at least one trick in spades no matter how evenly they are divided. For that reason you might lose the trick early in order to retain control later. Instead of playing the ace, king, and then a little one, you could simply play a little one first and then the ace and king.

Here is a similar situation, where the cards are the same but they are divided 5-3 between your hand and dummy:

DUMMY

♠ A K 4 3 2

WEST   EAST

♠ 10 9   ♠ Q J 8

YOU

♠ 7 6 5

It would be positively criminal simply to settle for two tricks with a beautiful suit like this. You have eight cards; they have five. One of them must have three cards, so you know you must lose a trick. What you can do is lead the five and when West plays the nine play the two from the dummy. Then the next time you get the lead, you will play your ace and king from dummy, which will take away the remaining spades from East and West. Dummy's four and three will then be high because they will be the only spades in play.

What is the difference between giving them the first trick and giving them the second or third trick? Very little. You still take four tricks in either case, but as long as you have a sure loser anyway, ducking early is advisable because it allows you to retain control later.

Note this: If you play the ace and king and then a little one, East will win the third trick with the queen, and you will have two good spades in dummy but no more spades in your hand. This means that in order to use your two good spades, you must have a way of getting over to dummy in another suit. But if you play a low spade first and then the ace and king, you are right where you want to be—in the dummy—and you can lead your two little spades without having to get over there in another suit. (Again, I say you should be practicing this with the cards in front of you.)

Lest you think you are giving away tricks to the opponents for nothing, you should realize that whenever you duck a trick (that is, play a low card from both hands), you would have had to lose a trick in that suit regardless.

Examine this one:

DUMMY

♠ 4 3 2

YOU

♠ A K 8 7 6 5

Now you have nine cards, which means the opponents have only four. Those four cards might easily be divided 2-2, in which case, after you played the ace and king, the four small ones in your hand would all be good. If it turned out that one opponent had three cards and the other only one, then—and only then— would you have to give them a trick in order to establish the remainder of your smaller cards.

Now you are ready to look at some of these longer suits that are built into bridge hands. Your job is getting a little more complex. These are the steps I want you to follow when you study the following hands:

(1)   Know how many tricks you need to make your contract.

(2)   Count up your sure tricks.

(3)   Look to see if you can establish any extra tricks by driving out an ace or an ace and a king.

(4)   Look to see if there is any chance of establishing some small cards in your long suits.

(5)   Decide which suit you are going to attack first and how many extra tricks you will probably get from that suit. (Getting pretty mean, aren't I?)

(a) DUMMY

♠ 3 2
♡ A 4 3
◇ A 9 8 7 6
♣ 4 3 2

YOU

♠ A K 4
♡ K 5 2
◇ K 4 3 2
♣ A 7 6

(b) DUMMY

♠ A 4 3
♡ K 5 4
◇ A 7 6 5
♣ K 5 4

YOU

♠ K Q 2
♡ A 7 3
◇ 4 3 2
♣ A 7 6 3

(c) DUMMY
♠ A 7 6
♡ K 3
◊ 9 7 6 5 4 3
♣ A 2

YOU
♠ K Q 5
♡ A 9 8
◊ 10 8 2
♣ K Q 4 3

Your final contract is 3 NT in each of the hands. The opening lead is the jack of spades on all three hands. Plan your play.

Solutions

(a) You have seven sure tricks and you should set up the diamonds immediately. You have nine diamonds between the two hands, leaving the opponents only four. You should play the king and ace of diamonds. If both opponents follow, all of your diamonds are good and you will take ten tricks. If one opponent started with three diamonds, you would concede a diamond but you would make four diamond tricks for a grand total of nine tricks coming to you. Notice you are establishing before taking your sure tricks.

(b) You have eight sure tricks and a chance for a ninth in either clubs or diamonds, both suits in which you have seven cards. As your clubs are stronger than your diamonds, you should try to establish your clubs with the hope that the opponents' clubs are divided 3-3. You can either play the king, ace, and a third club, or you can duck a club and then play the king and ace. (High card from short side.) If the clubs do divide 3-3, you make the hand. If not, you are in trouble.

(c) You have eight sure tricks, and you should see that the *only* suit from which you can get any extra tricks is diamonds. You cannot establish your fourth club because you only have six clubs between the two hands, divided 4-2. One of your opponents must have four clubs, so you can forget about that suit. You should simply lead a diamond every time you have the lead and hope that your opponents' diamonds are divided 2-2. In that case you will have established four additional tricks for yourself. Even if their diamonds are divided 3-1, you can lose three tricks in diamonds and still make three for yourself. But you must start establishing early.

KEY POINTERS

(1)   Your most important single asset in the majority of hands that you play is your long suit. And the longer the better.

(2)   Long suits can be established simply by playing the suit so many times that your opponents run out of the suit. In that case all of your smaller cards become good.

(3)   Any seven-card suit you hold can be established if the opponent's cards divide evenly for you.

(4)   If you and you partner have eight or more cards total in any one suit, you can usually make an extra trick or two in that suit by attacking it early.

(5)   If you are establishing a suit in which you know that one trick must be lost, you can duck a trick early (play a low card from both hands) and then play your ace and king. This is done to retain control and to eliminate entry problems.

(6)   Don't be afraid of long suits that do not have high cards in them. By leading them once, twice, or even three times, you will exhaust your opponents in that suit and make your remaining small cards good.

(7)   Set up your long suits before taking your sure tricks.

4
Taking Tricks by Finessing

♠ ♡ ◇ ♣

Well, there is still another way of getting yourself some tricks. You can finesse. The sad part about finessing is that most players (even those who have played for many years) do not understand it. But you will. First an example:

DUMMY

♠ K 5

YOU

♠ A 2

Let's go back to your sure trick count. If you were playing this hand and you wanted to take two tricks in spades, you could lead a low spade to the king or play the ace first and then the king; or if the lead happened to be in the dummy, you could take two tricks by leading low to the ace or leading the king and then low to the ace. In other words, it doesn't matter in this case which hand has the lead. But now look at this:

DUMMY

♠ K 5

WEST　　　　　**EAST**

?　　　　　　　?

YOU

♠ 3 2

Let's say you want to take a trick with the king. If you lead the king, one of your opponents will take the trick with the ace, and you wind up with nothing. How do you take tricks in suits that are missing some of the honors? *You must lead towards the honor with which you wish to take the trick. In other words, the lead must always come from the hand opposite the honor.*

Let's say you lead your two of spades. Presumably you don't know which of your opponents has the ace. Now you must start to do some imagining. Imagine that West has the ace and is the second one to play. If he plays the ace, your king will be good next time. If he plays low your king will take the trick. Therefore, if *West* has the ace, the king must eventually take a trick. Now imagine that East has the ace. You lead a low spade and West plays a low spade; then you play your king and East takes the trick with the ace. What happened?

What happened is that when you finessed (led towards) the king, it worked when West had the ace and didn't work when East had the ace. It is for that reason that finesses are fifty-fifty propositions. But in order to get your full fifty percent of the chance, you must lead *towards* your broken strength. Otherwise you will never take tricks with your stray kings, queens, and jacks.

Let's take the most common finesse of all:

DUMMY

♠ 5 4

WEST   EAST

?   ?

YOU

♠ A Q

Here you want to take a second trick with your queen. If you lead the queen from your own hand, somebody will take the trick with the king. So you must lead towards the queen. (And you must get to the dummy in another suit in order to lead the first spade from the dummy hand.) You lead the four and East plays low; then you finesse the queen. If East has the king, the queen takes the trick; if West has the king, your queen loses and you make only one trick—but at least you tried.

And don't worry about East playing the king when you lead low from dummy. You simply take it with the ace, and then the queen is automatically good.

Finesses can be repeated. Take a look at this (and this is

one lesson for which you definitely should be laying out the cards
in order to follow the diagrams we are studying here):

> DUMMY
> ♠ A Q J
> ♡ 2

WEST   EAST
♠ K 10 9   ♠ 8 7 6
♡ 10   ♡ 8

> YOU
> ♠ 5 4 3
> ♡ A

In studying finesses you must use a little imagination. Imagine, if you will, that these are the last four cards in everyone's
hands and that spades have never been played. You have the
lead and would like to take all of the remaining tricks. You
remember that in order to take tricks with kings, queens, and
jacks in suits which are not solid, you must lead towards those
cards. (If you have all the good tricks in a suit, the suit is called
solid, and it doesn't matter which hand you are in.)

So you lead a low spade from your hand, and West, who can
see the dummy, plays the nine. You don't know who has the
king, but you attempt a finesse by playing the queen (or the
jack). And what do you know, it works! East plays the six, so
you know that West must have the king. At this point you are
down to three cards in each hand:

> DUMMY
> ♠ A J
> ♡ 2

WEST   EAST
♠ K 10   ♠ 8 7
♡ 10   ♡ 8

> YOU
> ♠ 5 4
> ♡ A

The lead—and this is very important—is in the dummy hand. You would like to take a trick with the jack of spades. If you lead the ace, West will simply play the ten, and then his king—not your jack—will be good.

You must remember that to finesse a card is to lead towards that card. So you play the two of hearts over to your ace, and then you lead a spade from your hand. West plays the ten (it would do him no good to play the king, because you would take it with the ace), and you finesse the jack. After that you lead the ace and have successfully repeated your spade finesse.

Now what would have happened if your finesse had lost? Let's go back to the original four-card position:

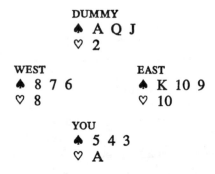

DUMMY
♠ A Q J
♡ 2

WEST
♠ 8 7 6
♡ 8

EAST
♠ K 10 9
♡ 10

YOU
♠ 5 4 3
♡ A

Once again you lead a low spade from your hand and finesse the queen from dummy. This time East takes the trick with the king, leaving you with the ace and jack in dummy, both of which are good. Now if you want to take tricks with your ace and jack, you don't have to lead towards them, because they now constitute solid strength. What we are getting at is this: if you are no longer missing any key honors in a suit, you no longer have to lead towards your honors; it is only when you are missing an honor that you have to finesse. You *were* missing the king, but once it has been played, you can take your tricks freely.

Let's take a look at some very common finessing positions before playing any hands:

DUMMY

♠ A J 2

WEST   EAST

?   ?

YOU

♠ K 4 3

Here you are missing the queen. You know you can take two tricks with the ace and the king, but you are itching to take a trick with dummy's jack as well. What do you think you should do?

Just remember the general rule. Whenever you want to take a trick with a lower honor, lead from the opposite hand. Don't lead the honor; lead towards it. (There are times when you will be leading an honor, but they are rare; most of the time you lead towards the honor with which you wish to take the trick.

So what you should do is this: if the lead is in the dummy, you should lead the two over to the king and then lead the three and finesse the jack. You can only hope that West has the queen. If the lead is in your hand, you should play the king (on the off chance that East has the queen all alone), and if not, finesse the jack.

Here is a similar one:

DUMMY

♠ A 4 3

WEST   EAST

?   ?

YOU

♠ Q 5 2

The lead is in your hand, and you would like to take two tricks in this suit. You know your ace is always good but you would like to make an additional trick with your queen. What should you do?

You should lead *towards* your queen. Lead a spade to the ace and then a low spade back. If East has the king, your queen must take a second trick. If West has the king, he will take your queen but, once again, at least you have tried.

Now you try some: decide which hand you should lead from and who must have the missing honor in order for your finesse to work. (West is to your left and East is to your right.)

(a)	DUMMY K Q 4	(b)	DUMMY 3	(c)	DUMMY A Q 3	(d)	DUMMY 6 5 3
	YOU 7 3 2		YOU A K J		YOU 7 5 2		YOU K Q J

Solutions

(a) You should lead low from your hand towards the king and hope that West has the ace. If the king wins, you must come back to your hand (in a different suit) and lead low towards the queen.

(b) You must lead low from the dummy hand and finesse the jack. You are hoping that East has the queen.

(c) Low from your hand and finesse the queen. You are hoping that West has the king.

(d) Here it doesn't matter which hand you lead from because you have all of the honors except the ace. You can lead the king from your hand or lead towards the king. The most you can make is two tricks, and you don't really care who has the ace. Compare this with the first example, where you must lead up to your king and queen because you don't have the jack.

Sometimes when finessing you are missing two honors. No matter—the principle is still the same. Lead towards your broken strength.

DUMMY

♠ A J 10

WEST   EAST

♠ Q 8 7 6   ♠ K 9 5

YOU

♠ 4 3 2

Let's pretend that this was the original distribution of the spade suit. You wish to take two tricks in the suit. First you lead low and finesse the jack, and it loses to the king.

Later you can repeat the finesse by returning to your hand and finessing the ten. If the opponents' honors are divided, you will take two tricks. If East has both the king and queen and both of your finesses lose, it just wasn't your day and you better be careful when you cross the street.

When would you ever lead an honor instead of leading towards an honor? This is a tough one. You must study these two diagrams very carefully:

(1) DUMMY   (2) DUMMY

♠ A 3 2   ♠ A 3 2

YOU   YOU

♠ Q 5 4   ♠ Q J 10

In both cases you would like to take some extra tricks besides your ace. In the first case you would lead towards your queen and hope that East had the king, but in the second you should lead the queen and hope West has the king. What is the difference? Why should we lead the queen in one case and lead towards it in the other?

Naturally, we have a rule to cover this situation, but I'm afraid if you merely memorize the rule without understanding the reason you will forget it when you begin to play—and you can't refer to a book when you are playing a hand.

Let's start with the reason. Whenever you are toying with the idea of leading an honor as opposed to leading towards it, you must always ask yourself one question: *If I lead an honor and the next player covers the honor with a higher honor will I have gained anything?*

Now let's look at the first diagram. If you lead the queen and West covers it with the king, you will have gained nothing. All you have left is your ace.

But in the second diagram if you lead your queen and West covers it with the king, you can take the king with the ace and you will have *promoted* the jack and ten to sure tricks.

Therefore, the rule when leading honors is: *In order to lead an honor rather than towards the honor, you must be able to promote at least one extra trick if your honor card is covered.* In essence this means that you do not lead queens, jacks, and tens (tens are considered honors) unless you have, between the two hands, the honor equal to (that is, directly below) the one you are leading or preferably two honors equal to the one you are leading. Don't lead a queen unless you have at least the jack and preferably the jack and ten to back it up. Don't lead a jack unless you have the ten or preferably the ten and nine to back it up.

Now we can discuss finesses a little more intelligently. Let's try these for size:

(a)   DUMMY   (b)   DUMMY   (c)   DUMMY
      A K 3 2   A 5 4 3   A K 2

      YOU   YOU   YOU
      J 6 5 4   Q J 10 9   J 10 3

        (d)   DUMMY   (e)   DUMMY
            A 6 5   A 8 7 6 5

            YOU   YOU
            J 10 9   Q 4 3 2

What would be the best way to play these card combinations?

Solutions

(a)   Lead the ace and the king and then lead to the jack if the queen has not already dropped. Do not lead the jack, because you do not have the ten.

(b)   Lead the queen. If West has the king but does not choose to cover, your queen will win, and you can repeat the finesse. If West covers (the true test), you will take it with the ace, and your jack, ten, and nine will have been promoted.

(c)   Lead the jack and let it ride (that is, play low from dummy) if West plays low. If West covers the jack with the queen (the test), you will have promoted your ten.

(d)   Lead the jack. If West covers, you win it with the ace, and then you can force out the other honor easily. If West plays low and your jack loses, you must return to your hand and lead the ten. If West covers the ten, you will have promoted your nine.

(e)   Lead the ace and then lead low to your queen. You must not lead the queen, because you do not have the lower honors; if you led the queen and she were covered, you would not have promoted anything.

Now let's look at some of these finessable combinations in a bridge hand. How would you plan the following 3 NT hands? In all four cases you have received the lead of the queen of spades.

(a)   DUMMY
   ♠ A 3 2
   ♡ K 3 2
   ◇ Q J 10 9
   ♣ A 3 2

   YOU
   ♠ K 5 4
   ♡ A 7 6
   ◇ A 4 3 2
   ♣ 9 8 7

(b)   DUMMY
   ♠ A 5 4
   ♡ J 7 6
   ◇ Q 3 2
   ♣ A 7 6 5

   YOU
   ♠ K 7 6
   ♡ Q 5
   ◇ A K J 4
   ♣ Q 4 3 2

(c)   DUMMY   (d)   DUMMY
      ♠ 3 2   ♠ 7 6 5
      ♡ 7 6 5   ♡ A Q J 10
      ◊ A Q J 10 9   ◊ 4 3 2
      ♣ 4 3 2   ♣ A Q 5

      YOU   YOU
      ♠ A K 4   ♠ A 4 3 2
      ♡ A K J   ♡ 7 6 5
      ◊ 4 3 2   ◊ A K Q J
      ♣ J 10 7 6   ♣ 4 3 2

Solutions

(a)   You have five sure tricks outside of diamonds, the
      suit you are going to have to establish. It isn't a bad
      idea to count your sure tricks outside of the suit you
      are going to set up (establish) in order to see how
      many tricks you do need in the suit you are setting
      up. You need four tricks in diamonds. You are miss-
      ing only the king, and you cannot afford to lose a
      trick in the suit. You are fortunate to have the jack
      and ten as well. You should win the spade lead in
      dummy and then play the queen of diamonds. You
      are hoping East has the king. If West has the king,
      well, there will always be another hand.

(b)   You have six sure tricks outside of clubs, the suit you
      are going to establish. You need to make three club
      tricks, and fortunately, you have eight clubs between
      your hand and the dummy. You are going to have to
      try to make a trick with your queen as well as with
      one of your smaller clubs. Remember, the small clubs
      will be good when the opponents don't have any more.
      Your proper play is to win the spade in either hand
      (some plays are optional), then play the ace of clubs,
      and then lead a low club towards the queen, hoping
      East has the king. If he does, your queen will be good
      and your little one also if your opponents' clubs were
      divided 3-2, the most probable division.

(c) You have four sure tricks outside of diamonds, so you will need to take five tricks in diamonds. You are missing the king, and you should lead towards your broken strength. Your proper play is to win the spade lead with the ace and then immediately lead a low diamond and finesse the queen. If the queen loses to the king, you will have established four diamond tricks, but that will still leave you one short. It then will become necessary to lead a low heart from the dummy hand to finesse the jack for your ninth trick. However, if the diamond finesse works, you should come back to your hand with the ace of hearts and repeat the diamond finesse. As a general rule, you finesse in your longer suits before your shorter ones because you can establish more tricks in your longer suits than you can in your shorter ones.

(d) Here you have six sure tricks outside of your heart suit, which is the suit you should select to establish. Notice that it becomes a little more difficult to estimate the number of sure tricks we have in suits which require finesses. We do not know whether or not the finesses are going to work! For example, on this hand we do not know whether we can take one or two tricks in clubs. It depends upon the location of the king. The same is true in hearts. We might take all four heart tricks or, if the finesse doesn't work, only three. So the thing to do is to count your sure tricks outside of these touchy suits to see how many tricks you need in your finessable ones. As it is better to finesse in longer suits, we would simply count one trick in clubs temporarily and concentrate on hearts, our longest suit. We would win the ace of spades and then lead a low heart and finesse the queen. If the finesse loses, we will have established three extra heart tricks and enough to make our contract. If the finesse wins, we can come back to our hand with a diamond to repeat the finesse in hearts. Now maybe you can see why it is better not to use the diamonds prematurely. They can be used as entry cards when you are finessing in other suits. It may be necessary to finesse hearts three times. What if the original heart distribution was:

DUMMY

A Q J 10

WEST   EAST

K 4 3 2   9 8

YOU

7 6 5

You lead low to the queen and that wins. Now you must come back to your hand and lead low to the jack. After the jack wins, you must come back to your hand and finesse the ten. Play this out, and you will see why your diamonds are so important as re-entries to your hand.

KEY POINTERS

(1)   *Solid strength* (A K Q facing x x x) tricks can be taken by leading from either hand first.

(2)   With *broken strength* you must initiate the lead from the hand opposite the broken strength.

(3)   Broken strength can become solid strength! Let's say you have A Q J facing x x x. If you finesse and lose the trick, you then have solid strength and can take the remainder of the tricks by leading from either hand.

(4)   Do not lead a queen, jack, or ten unless you have equal honor cards to back it up. You must have at least one honor equal to the one you are leading; preferably two between your hand and dummy.

(5)   As a general rule, when counting sure tricks, count your sure tricks outside of the suit you plan to establish. Then you will know how many tricks you need in your key suit.

(6)   If you must take a finesse, take it in a long suit. In

that way you are at least setting up your smaller cards in case the finesse loses.

(7)   Remember that finesses are only fifty-fifty propositions and that the majority of your tricks will still come from length. However, very often your long suit will require a finesse or two in order to establish it.

5

The Hold-Up Play

♠ ♡ ◇ ♣

Has it occurred to you that while you have been so busy taking, establishing, and finessing for extra tricks, we haven't given any thought to your opponents? Unfortunately, they are there. Not only are they there but they are trying to do the same thing you are—namely, establish tricks for themselves.

Surely you remember how easy it was to establish tricks when we had

DUMMY
♠ x x x

YOU
♠ K Q J 10

All we did was lead the king and drive out the ace to set up three tricks for ourselves. Right? Well, what if they have the K Q J 10? All they have to do is lead the king and drive out our ace, and they will have established three tricks for themselves. Besides, they have the opening lead, so they can begin to establish their best suit before we can begin ours. The opening lead is so valuable and important to the defensive side that entire books have been written about selecting the proper opening lead!

If the defender who happens to have the opening lead is fortunate enough to have a suit like K Q J 10, he won't have to read a whole book about selecting the proper lead. He will simply plunk down his king and keep playing the suit until the ace is removed, making good all the rest of his cards in that suit.

You, as the declarer, must be able to put a stop to this or

else you won't make too many of your notrump contracts. Fortunately, you sometimes have a counter to your opponents' establishing their long suit. It is called a *hold-up play*. Study this next
diagram very carefully:

DUMMY
♠ 3 2

WEST
♠ K Q J 10 9

EAST
♠ 8 7 6

YOU
♠ A 5 4

Let's assume that you are playing a notrump contract and
that West, who has the opening lead, starts out with the king of
spades. You, sitting South, hold the ace, which in notrump is a
perfect card simply because it can never be lost and you can use
it whenever you like.

You can take the first trick; or you can allow the king to win
and take the second spade trick; or you can allow two spades to
win and take the third. What is the difference?

One colossal difference! If you take the first or second
spade, East remains with a spade. If you take the third spade,
East is left with no more spades. Why is that so important? Remember, in most notrump hands you do not have enough sure
tricks to make your contract, so you must establish. Establishing
means letting the opponents have the lead. If the opponents have,
in the meantime, established a suit of their own, you are going
to be in a little trouble.

Look at the diagram again. Once we relinquish our ace, the
opponents have an established spade suit. If you take either the
first or second spade trick and then let your opponents have the
lead in another suit, it won't matter which opponent leads: if it
is West, he will take his established spade tricks, and if it is East,
he will lead a spade over to West's established spades.

But if you take the third spade trick and then give up the
lead to East, *he will not have any more spades, and so West will
not be able to use the remainder of his good spades.*

The time has come to look at all four hands to see how this hold-up play works.

NORTH
♠ 3 2
♡ A 5 4
◇ A J 10 9 8
♣ K 5 4

WEST
♠ K Q J 10 9
♡ 9 8 7
◇ 5 4 2
♣ 9 8

EAST
♠ 8 7 6
♡ Q J 10
◇ K 7 6
♣ Q J 10 7

SOUTH
♠ A 5 4
♡ K 6 3 2
◇ Q 3
♣ A 6 3 2

(From now on in this book, you will always be South and dummy will always be North. This is the normal format for newspaper bridge columns; South always winds up playing the hand and invariably has the best hand.)

For a change you are in 3 NT! You may as well get used to playing hands at 3 NT. It is by far the most common contract and lends itself well to examples.

West leads the king of spades. You count your sure tricks, and you find that outside of diamonds, your main suit, you have five tricks. So you are going to have to establish at least four diamond tricks. You are missing the king, which means you might have to give up the lead in diamonds in order to realize your four tricks.

Whenever you are missing an ace in your best suit, you know you are going to have to give up the lead to establish any tricks for yourself. However, when you are missing only the king, you might not have to lose a trick at all. Instead, you might be able to take a winning finesse.

In this particular case you would lead the queen of diamonds from your hand and play low if West plays low. If West has the king of diamonds, you will not lose a diamond trick; if East has the king, you must lose one trick, but you will get four in return.

Bridge players have learned always to expect the worst. East might have the king of diamonds, and then what about the spades? Remember, West led a spade and drove out our ace. Now all of the opposing spades are good.

But you did not win the first or second spade trick. You took the third round of spades, and *then* you finessed the queen of diamonds. Sure enough, the finesse loses but East does not have any more spades to return, so West cannot use his two good spades.

Maybe now you can see what you have accomplished by winning the third round of spades. You have severed the communications between the East and West hands. You have cut their lifeline, which was spades.

Now let's take a look at another hand where you must establish tricks, but this time you must knock out an ace. It is going to look very similar to the last hand you played:

```
                    NORTH
                    ♠ 3 2
                    ♡ A 5 4
                    ◊ K J 10 9 2
                    ♣ K 5 4

WEST                                    EAST
♠ K Q J 10 9                            ♠ 8 7 6
♡ 9 8 7                                 ♡ Q J 10
◊ 5 4 3                                 ◊ A 8 7
♣ 9 8                                   ♣ Q J 10 7

                    SOUTH
                    ♠ A 5 4
                    ♡ K 6 3 2
                    ◊ Q 6
                    ♣ A 6 3 2
```

Once again you are in 3 NT and West leads the king of spades. This time you must establish your diamond suit, but you are missing the ace and don't know who has it. You do know, however, that you have only one stopper in spades and that you can take the trick whenever you wish.

Once again, when the opponents attack your weakest suit and you have only one stopper and *can take the trick whenever you wish,* you normally take the third round of the suit.

Let's see what happens if you win the third spade, discarding a heart from dummy, and immediately go about establishing your main suit. *You do not let the fact that the opponents have an established suit (spades) prevent you from establishing your own suit.*

You lead the queen of diamonds (high card from the short side) and continue the suit until the ace has been removed. If you are lucky, East, the hand we assume has no more spades, will have the ace of diamonds. If he does, he will not have a spade to lead over to West; if he does have a spade, it means that each opponent started with four spades and that you will only lose one more spade trick, for a total of three spade tricks and one diamond trick lost.

In this particular deal East has the ace of diamonds, and you will make your three notrump contract. But what if West has the ace of diamonds? Then you will not make your contract!

West will make good his ace of diamonds and his remaining spades, and you will be set. But this is no great shame; even in the strongest bridge games in the world, the declarer only makes a little more than half of his contracts. In other words, going down is nothing rare.

One of the lessons that a beginner must learn is that not every contract makes and that some perfectly good contracts are defeated merely because of a clever lead or because the wrong hand has a particular card. If you worry too much about getting set, you will end up taking all your sure tricks prematurely and losing the tricks you might have established. You must establish your tricks (if you don't have enough sure tricks for your contract) and let them take theirs—if they can.

But it won't be easy for them to take their tricks if you remember about this hold-up play.

Bear in mind one important fact about an ace: you can take it whenever you like—you can't lose it. But that doesn't always apply to a lower honor. Study this diagram:

NORTH

♠ 7 6

WEST   EAST

♠ A J 8 3 2   ♠ Q 10 4

SOUTH

♠ K 9 5

Pretend you are playing a notrump contract. West leads a low spade and East plays the queen. If you take the trick, you will have no further stopper or control in spades and, what's worse, both East and West will remain with spades, so that if either should get the lead in another suit you will lose four more spade tricks. So what should you do? You should play the king of spades at once!

Why? Well, if you duck the queen and don't play your king, as you would if your king were the ace, you will not make a single trick with your king. East will have the lead and will return the ten. If you play low, the ten will take the trick and then your king will go under West's ace. Covering the ten with the king won't work either because West is hovering over you with the ace. But before we make any blanket rules about holding up, let's look at this one:

NORTH

♠ 7 6

WEST   EAST

♠ Q 10 8 3 2   ♠ A J 4

SOUTH

♠ K 9 5

You are again in notrump. West leads a low spade in an effort to establish his long spade suit. East takes it with the ace and returns the jack. What should you do?

I hope you can see the difference between this diagram and the last. Now that the ace has been played, your king is *high*. You can't lose it! In this case it would be safe to hold up with the king and take the third spade. East would be exhausted in spades, and if he later got the lead, he might well have trouble giving the lead to West, who wants to take his good spade tricks.

Now let's see how you do on these problems:

(a)   NORTH
  ♠ 3 2
  ♡ K Q 5
  ◊ J 10 9 3 2
  ♣ 5 4 3

  SOUTH
  ♠ K 9 6
  ♡ A 3 2
  ◊ K Q 4
  ♣ A K 6 2

Contract: 3 NT

(a)   West leads the five of spades and East plays the jack. Do you take the trick?
(b)   How many sure tricks do you have?
(c)   Which suit are you going to establish?
(d)   Which card are you going to play in that suit?

(b)   NORTH
  ♠ A 6 4
  ♡ 7 3
  ◊ A 8 3 2
  ♣ K 6 5 4

  SOUTH
  ♠ K 3
  ♡ A 4 2
  ◊ K 6 5
  ♣ Q J 10 9 8

Contract: 3 NT

(a) West leads the queen of hearts. Do you take the trick?
(b) How many sure tricks do you have?
(c) Which suit are you going to establish and who do you
     hope has the key card in that suit? Why?

(c)   NORTH
            ♠ 5 4 2
            ♡ 7 3
            ◊ A K 7 5
            ♣ Q J 10 3

            SOUTH
            ♠ A 10 3
            ♡ J 8 4
            ◊ Q J 10 9
            ♣ A K 4

Contract: 3 NT

(a) West leads a low spade and East plays the jack. Do
     you take this trick? Why or why not?
(b) What is your plan?

Solutions

(a) You should take the trick. East, who is third to play
     to the first trick, will generally play his highest card
     when his partner has led a low card. Therefore, East's
     playing the jack probably means that he doesn't have
     the ace. So West probably has the ace, which means
     that if you don't grab your king right now, you will
     never get it.

     Even though you have no remaining stopper in
     spades, you should immediately attack the diamond
     suit by leading the king. You have six tricks outside
     of diamonds and you cannot arrive at nine tricks un-
     til you remove the ace of diamonds. It is true that
     when the opponents get in with the ace of diamonds,
     they will take their good spades. But remember, they
     only had eight spades between them originally. If they

had four each, they will now have three each and will only be able to take three tricks in the suit. What applies to you applies to them also: they cannot take more tricks in any given suit than the longer hand has cards. This means that if their spades were divided 4-4, you will only lose three more spade tricks in addition to the ace of diamonds. If their spades were divided 5-3, then you will lose four spades and the ace of diamonds, thus going down one trick. However, you must in any case attack the diamonds *before* you take your sure tricks in the other suits.

(b) This time you should hold up your ace of hearts until the third round. You have only five sure tricks outside of clubs, so you must establish that suit. You should hope that East has the ace of clubs, because West has the good hearts and you have probably exhausted East's hearts (and thus cut the connection between their hands) by holding up the ace of hearts.

(c) This time you should play the ace. There are two excellent reasons for *not* holding up. First and most important is that you have nine sure tricks which you can just take. *You have nothing to establish.* Second, you are even weaker in hearts than you are in spades. Your opponent might wake up and shift to hearts. Then where will you be? Remember, holding up is done primarily when you have to establish tricks. If you have them ready-made, don't be a hero—take the bloody things!

Finally, we come to an advanced type of hold-up play. Take a look at this diagram:

NORTH

♠ 5 4

WEST   EAST

♠ K Q 10 9 8   ♠ 7 3 2

SOUTH

♠ A J 6

West leads the king against your notrump contract. If you take the trick, you remain with the J 6. If East should get the lead later, he can lead through your jack, and you won't be able to make a trick with it. But if you duck the opening lead of the king, good things might happen. If West continues leading the suit into your remaining A J, you will take two tricks. If West shifts suits, you have retained your spade stopper and perhaps can establish some tricks in another suit without worrying about spades. This tactic of ducking with the ace and the jack when the king is led is called the Bath Coup, the origin of the term unknown.

KEY POINTERS

(1)   The *hold-up play* is used to great advantage in notrump to sever the communications in the opponents' best suit by taking the second or, more commonly, the third round of the suit when you only have one stopper in that suit.

(2)   The hold-up play is used when declarer has to establish a suit of his own. If he has enough sure tricks to make his contract, he need not make a hold-up play.

(3)   If declarer has a weaker suit than the one that has been led, it is usually wrong to make a hold-up play because the opponents might shift to the weaker suit.

(4)   Hold-up plays don't always work. The player who has the good tricks in the suit that has been led might also have the entry that declarer must knock out. However, if the partner of the opening leader has the entry, the hold-up play can be devastating.

(5)   Do not make hold-up plays with conditional stoppers like kings and queens if the higher cards in the suit are still outstanding. You will wind up losing your kings and queens.

(6)   However, if the ace has been played, your king is no longer a conditional stopper. It is always good and can be played when you please. In this case you may make a hold-up play.

(7)   Do not be afraid to establish tricks if the opponents have already established their suit first. They may not have enough tricks in their suit to defeat your contract, and even if

they do, you have no option but to establish your suit if you do not have enough sure tricks.

(8)   *Do not be afraid to go down. Do not be afraid to give up the lead.*

THE RULE OF ELEVEN

Now that you have mastered the hold-up play, the *rule of eleven* will seem like child's play in comparison. Nevertheless, it comes in handy so often that you should be familiar with it.

You have noticed, no doubt, that against notrump contracts in particular, the defenders usually lead their longest suit. The card that is led is determined by the original holding in the suit. If, for example, a sequence is held such as Q J 10 7 4, the top card is led, but if the opening leader does not have a sequence, the original fourth highest card is led. From holdings such as K J 8 6   A 9 7 6 3   or   J 8 7 6 4 3   the six would be the proper lead.

As declarer, you can put this knowledge to work. Assume for the moment that you are declarer in a notrump contract and that the opening lead by West is the eight of spades. This is what you see in spades between your hand and the dummy:

NORTH
♠ A Q 2

WEST   EAST
leads the   ?
eight

SOUTH
♠ 10 5 3

You assume that West is leading his fourth highest spade. (There are no certainties in this game.) This simply means that West has three spades higher than the eight. But how about East? How many spades does East have above the eight?

In order to determine the number of cards that the *partner* of the original leader holds above the one that has been led, we use the rule of eleven.

The rule: *Subtract the number of the card that has been led from the number eleven.* The answer will tell you the number of cards above the one that has been led that are outstanding in the remaining three hands (that is, excluding the original leader's hand).

Using the example above, subtract the card that was led from eleven. Being a student of higher mathematics, you should come up with three. Thus, there are three cards above the eight in the remaining three hands (North, South, and East). You can always see two of the remaining three hands, so you simply count the number of cards above the eight that you can see between your own hand and the dummy. In this case, since you can account for all three outstanding cards above the eight between your hand and the dummy, you can conclude that East has no card above the eight.

Using this knowledge you should play *low* from dummy and win the first trick with the ten! Later you can safely finesse the queen.

Let's uncover the mystery of the unseen hands:

NORTH

♠ A Q 2

WEST		EAST
♠ K J 9 8 4		♠ 7 6

SOUTH

♠ 10 5 3

That was so much fun that we'll try it again, but this time with the lead of a seven:

NORTH

♠ A K 2

WEST	EAST
leads the	?
seven	

SOUTH

♠ 10 9 3

West leads the seven of spades against your notrump contract, and you are going to apply the rule of eleven in order to discover how many cards East has above the seven. (You already know that West has three cards above the seven.)

So you go into your act. Subtract seven from eleven; the difference is four. *There are four cards higher than the seven in the remaining three hands.* You can see two in the dummy and two in your own hand. Therefore, East has no card higher than the seven; you can safely play low from dummy and take the trick with the nine or ten.

This was the complete layout:

NORTH

♠ A K 2

WEST   EAST

♠ Q J 8 7 4   ♠ 6 5

SOUTH

♠ 10 9 3

Now a word of caution. Only the declarer and the partner of the opening leader can apply the rule of eleven. The opening leader cannot make his opening lead and then apply the rule, because it is accurate only when applied to the three hands excluding his.

East, however, can and should apply the rule of eleven in order to find out how many cards the declarer holds above the one his partner has led.

Let's go back to our first example. West led the eight. Put yourself in the East position:

NORTH

♠ A Q 2

WEST   EAST

leads the   ♠ 7 6

eight

SOUTH

?

As East you would think to yourself, "Eight from eleven is three; there are three cards higher than the eight in the remaining three hands. I can see two in the dummy and I have none. Therefore, declarer has one card higher than the eight." When declarer plays that card, you know that he has played his only card higher than the eight.

Let's go back to the declarer's seat again:

NORTH

♠ A J 10

WEST   EAST

leads the   ?

six

SOUTH

♠ 8 3 2

West leads the six of spades. (I once gave a lecture on the rule of eleven and used only spades as my example suit. After the lesson a lady wanted to know if the rule worked if any other suit was led!) Your job is to figure out how many spades higher than the six East had originally.

The mental processes should be: (1) six from eleven is five, (2) there are five cards higher than the six in the three remaining hands, (3) I can see three of those five cards in the dummy and I have one in my own hand, (4) therefore, East has one card higher than the six.

Now it is true that you don't know which card it is, but let's assume for the sake of the example that you play the jack from the dummy and East takes the trick with the queen. Who has the king? West must have the king because the rule told us that East had only one card above the six, and he has already played it.

Now let's see what the whole suit was originally:

NORTH

♠ A J 10

WEST   EAST

♠ K 9 7 6 4   ♠ Q 5

SOUTH

♠ 8 3 2

Let's check the rule from the East position. East can see four cards above the six between his hand and the dummy, which means that the declarer has exactly one card above the six. *The rule never lies,* provided that the original leader of the suit is leading his fourth highest card.

Perhaps you have noticed that some of the time the term opening leader is being used, and at other times, the original leader. The reason is that the rule works not only on opening lead but any time a suit is led *for the first time* (provided, again, that a fourth highest card is led):

```
                    NORTH
                    ♠ Q 4 3

        WEST                    EAST
         ?                      leads the
                                seven

                    SOUTH
                    ♠ K 10 2
```

You are South, playing a notrump contract, but this time West leads a heart, and East takes the trick and shifts to a spade. You may apply the rule of eleven whenever a new suit is led— regardless of when the first lead is made and regardless of which defender makes the lead.

In this case, subtracting seven from eleven tells you that there are four cards higher than the seven in the remaining three hands (South, North, and West).

You can see two cards above the seven in your own hand and one in the dummy, which means that West, the partner of the original leader, has one card above the seven. Assume that you play the ten and that West produces the jack. Who has the ace? East must have the ace because West had only one card above the seven and you have already seen it. You should take the trick with the queen, and later you will take a second trick with the king.

This was the layout:

NORTH
♠ Q 4 3

WEST   EAST
♠ J 6   ♠ A 9 8 7 5

SOUTH
♠ K 10 2

Perhaps you are thinking that leading the fourth highest card helps declarer too much. In some cases it does, but in others it helps the partner of the original leader even more. Stick with your fourth best leads and don't worry about it. Most declarers are too lazy to even use the rule.

As desirable as fourth best leads are, there will be times when you will not be leading from your longest suit on defense but will be leading from a short suit, say 8 5 3. So you lead the eight—*top of nothing*. (When holding three worthless cards the top card is usually led, hence the expression "top of nothing.") Let's see what kind of havoc this causes for a declarer who is religiously using "the rule."

NORTH
♠ A Q 2

WEST   EAST
leads the
eight   ?

SOUTH
♠ 10 5 3

This was our first example, in which we decided that East had no card higher than the eight and we played low expecting to take the trick with the ten. But wait! When we play low, East produces an apparition—the jack!

What should we do? Abandon the rule forever? No, don't abandon the rule. West has simply decided not to lead from a long suit. He is no doubt leading top of nothing and now we know it. Not only does East have the jack but very likely the king as well. It can happen. Don't panic if the rule doesn't work.

Simply reconsider the lead. It may be top of three small cards or even top of a doubleton.

Another point: When a very low card is led, such as the deuce, three, or four, the rule of eleven will still work, of course, but you will generally find that the information you obtain won't help you as much. As a beginner, you should probably use the rule only if a five, six, seven, or eight is led. (The lead of a nine or higher is never fourth best, so there is no point in using the rule when any of these cards is led.)

Quiz time. On the four problems that follow you will be the declarer in the South position. Your job will be to use the rule of eleven and to decide in each case (1) how many cards above the one being led your right-hand opponent (East) has and (2) on the basis of that information, which card you should play from dummy.

(a)

NORTH
♠ A K J 2

WEST
*leads the
seven*

EAST
?

SOUTH
♠ 9 6 3

(b)

NORTH
♠ K 10 2

WEST
*leads the
six*

EAST
?

SOUTH
♠ A 9 3

(c)

NORTH
♠ Q J 9

WEST
*leads the
five*

EAST
?

SOUTH
♠ A 7 3

(d)   NORTH
                        ♠ A K 2

            WEST   EAST
            leads the   ?
            eight

                        SOUTH
                        ♠ J 10 9

Solutions

(a)   Using "the rule," we discover that East has no card
      higher than the seven; therefore, our first play from
      the dummy should be the deuce. This is the layout:

                        NORTH
                        ♠ A K J 2

            ♠ Q 10 8 7 5   EAST
            WEST   ♠ 4

                        SOUTH
                        ♠ 9 6 3

      You can take it with the nine and by finessing the
      jack later, take all four tricks.

(b)   Using the rule of eleven, you discover that East has
      exactly one card higher than the six. You should play
      low from dummy and wait to see what that card is.
      If it is an honor, you can capture it. Later you can
      safely finesse the ten through West because you know
      that East had only one card higher than the six
      originally. (If East's higher card were the seven or
      eight, you would simply take the first trick with the
      nine. The layout:

                        NORTH
                        ♠ K 10 2

            WEST   EAST
            ♠ Q 8 7 6 5   ♠ J 4

                        SOUTH
                        ♠ A 9 3

(c)   This time you know that East has one card higher than the five. You should play the queen from dummy. If East plays the king, you take it with the ace, and later you can safely finesse dummy's nine. If the queen holds, you can be pretty sure that West has the king, in which case you should try to keep East from leading through your ace over to West's king:

NORTH
♠ Q J 9

WEST
♠ K 8 6 5 2

EAST
♠ 10 4

SOUTH
♠ A 7 3

(d)   What happened? There should be only three cards above the eight in the remaining three hands, and you can see five between your hand and the dummy! West is not leading fourth best, the sneak. Whenever there are more cards above the one led than there should be according to "the rule," it simply means that a fourth best card was not led. Apparently West has decided to lead top of nothing, and this is probably the layout:

NORTH
♠ A K 2

WEST
♠ 8 4 3

EAST
♠ Q 7 6 5

SOUTH
♠ J 10 9

In this case your best play would be to take the trick in dummy and try to prevent West from leading the suit a second time. The best way to do that is to take all of your finesses into East and hopefully prevent West from getting the lead. (In the following chapter you will see how to prevent a particular opponent from getting the lead and how to take your finesses "into a particular hand.")

KEY POINTERS

(1)   The lead of a low spot-card, particularly against no-trump contracts, is usually a fourth highest lead. If that card is either the five, six, seven, or eight, the *rule of eleven* should be applied.

(2)   The rule of eleven is simply this: Declarer (or partner of the opening leader) subtracts the card led from eleven. The answer tells him how many cards above the one led are out in the *remaining* three hands—that is, outside of the opening leader's hand. Declarer can always see the dummy and his own hand and thus can ascertain the number of cards higher than the one led in his right-hand opponent's hand.

(3)   This rule can be applied any time at all during the play of the hand, provided that the opponent is leading his fourth best card and that it is the first time the suit is being led.

(4)   At times it will be apparent that the opening lead is not a fourth best card. For example, any lead of a nine or higher is not a fourth best card, and the rule should not be used with such a lead. Another possibility is that the rule will tell you, for example, that there are four cards higher than the one led in the remaining three hands and you will be able to see five cards higher. This simply means that the opening leader is not leading fourth best and may be leading top of nothing. You will learn more about these leads in the chapter on defensive play.

(5)   The rule of eleven is applicable against suit contracts, but one must take care since short suit leads are much more common against suit contracts, and, therefore, the rule will not be applicable nearly so often as it will against a notrump contract.

(6)   *The rule never lies if a fourth best card is led.*

6

The Danger Hand

♠ ♡ ◇ ♣

You have now arrived at the turning point in your notrump career. You are going to be asked to watch *their* cards a little more closely and to imagine the bad things that can happen to you!

First things first. Let's go back to our hold-up manoeuvre, which should be kindergarten stuff for you by now:

NORTH

♠ 6 5

WEST   EAST

♠ K Q J 10 9   ♠ 8 7 4

SOUTH

♠ A 3 2

You, South, are playing a notrump contract, and West leads the king of spades. You dutifully win the third round of the suit leaving West with two good spades and East with none. We now can safely say that West is the *danger hand,* because if he should ever get the lead in another suit, he has good tricks to take. And East is the *non-danger hand,* because he has no more spades and if he should get the lead in another suit, he could not harm you in spades.

The point is this: how do you know that it is West who still has the good spades and not East? How do you know the situation wasn't like this?

NORTH

♠ 6 5

WEST　　　　　　　　　　　　　EAST

♠ K Q J　　　　　　　♠ 10 9 8 7 4

SOUTH

♠ A 3 2

In this case, after the third round of spades, East becomes the danger hand, because he remains with the good spades, while West is the non-danger hand. The answer to our question is that you can't always tell which opponent remains with the good cards. But you usually can.

The clues are the bidding and the size of the card led. If, for example, East has bid spades and West leads a spade, you must conclude that East has the longer spades.

If there has been no bidding to guide you, you usually assume that the person who leads the suit has the length, because it is normal to lead from length at notrump. Once in a while if an eight or a nine is led against your notrump contract, you might conclude that the opening leader is leading from a short suit and trying to find some length in his partner's hand.

Since low cards and honor cards are generally led from long suit holdings, the lead of an eight or a nine tends to be from a short suit.

Now we will study a somewhat more complicated example of the danger hand. Read this carefully and try to understand it—the future happiness of many of your partners depends on this! Take a careful look at the diagram:

NORTH

♠ 7 5 4

WEST　　　　　　　　　　　　　EAST

♠ A Q 9 3 2　　　　　♠ 10 8

SOUTH

♠ K J 6

Once again, you are playing a notrump contract. West leads the three of spades, a low card, indicating strength. You play low from the dummy, East plays the ten, and you take the trick with the jack. This is what remains:

                      NORTH
                      ♠ 7 5

WEST   EAST
♠ A Q 9 2   ♠ 8

                      SOUTH
                      ♠ K 6

What data do you have at your disposal? You know that West has strength in the suit because he has led a low card. East, third to play, is supposed to play his highest card when his partner leads a low card and dummy has no honors in the suit. Therefore, East has neither the ace nor the queen. He has denied this by his play of the ten.

Now you know that West is hovering over your king with the ace and the queen. So who is the danger hand? West? Wrong! East is the danger hand!

Before I explain this, let's have a good definition of the danger hand. *The danger hand is the hand which, if it gets the lead, can hurt you in one of two ways: (1) by taking good tricks in a suit or suits which you no longer have protected or (2) by leading through one of your honor cards over to a higher honor or honors in his partner's hand.*

Now let's go back to our spade holding. We have taken the first trick with the jack and now the cards look like this:

                      NORTH
                      ♠ 7 5

WEST   EAST
♠ A Q 9 2   ♠ 8

                      SOUTH
                      ♠ K 6

If *West* should get the lead in another suit and continue spades, you must take a trick with the king no matter which spade West leads. But if East should get the lead in another suit and return the eight of spades, West will take four more spade tricks, and you will not make a second trick with your king. In this case, therefore, it is East that is the danger hand, not West.

Because the opponents have the nasty habit of leading your weakest suit when you play a notrump hand and because you cannot always hold up, you will frequently have to determine which opponent is the danger hand while you still retain an honor card in the suit led.

Before we discuss what to do about a danger hand, let's look at a third situation which is very similar to the preceding one. Let's pretend that you started with this in spades but that the opponents have led a different suit:

NORTH

♠ 3 2

WEST   EAST

?   ?

SOUTH

♠ K 5

You are not very strong in spades; at most you have one stopper. You do not know who has the ace but this is what you should be thinking:

"Phew! They didn't lead a spade, so I'm temporarily safe. If the ace of spades is in the East hand, I will make one spade trick no matter which of my opponents leads spades. But if West has the ace of spades and East leads through my king, I won't take a single trick in spades and the opponents will take oodles of spades. Therefore, East is the danger hand, because *he could conceivably lead through my king of spades*. On the other hand, if West leads a spade, I will take a trick with my king."

In order to see how we cope with the two danger-hand situations, we must look at an entire hand:

NORTH
♠ 7 5
♡ A Q J
◇ A Q J 10 4
♣ 9 8 7

WEST
♠ K J 8 6 4
♡ 9 8 5 2
◇ 5 3
♣ K 6

EAST
♠ Q 10 9
♡ 10 6 4 3
◇ K 7 6
♣ 5 4 3

SOUTH
♠ A 3 2
♡ K 7
◇ 9 8 2
♣ A Q J 10 2

Once again, you are playing 3 NT and West leads the six of spades. (Opponents don't always lead spades, by the way.) East plays the queen (third hand high), and you decide to make a hold-up play and take the third round of the suit, discarding a club from dummy.

At this point the opponents have two spades remaining and you think that West has them because he was the original leader of the spade suit. Therefore, West is the danger hand. This doesn't mean that you give West the evil eye at the table; you simply try to prevent him from getting the lead.

You count your sure tricks. You have one spade, three hearts, one club, and one diamond: a total of six sure tricks. You must establish three more tricks, and you have two suits to choose from: clubs and diamonds. Either of these suits will give you four tricks even if you lose the finesse to the king.

Which suit should you go at first? Let's take a closer look at these two suits, which look so much alike. In diamonds you would lead the nine and play low, finessing the king into the East hand. In other words, if the diamond finesse loses, East is the one that takes the trick. If West has the king of diamonds, it is caught between your hand and the dummy. In clubs, the opposite occurs. If you enter dummy with a heart in order to lead the nine of clubs and finesse the club, the club finesse goes into the West hand, the danger hand.

Remember, West is the one with the good spades. So as long as you have a choice, you should take the finesse into the non-danger hand, East.

Let's say East takes the trick with the king of diamonds and returns a club. Now what should you do? The first thing you must do (on all notrump hands) after you have established a suit is to *recount your sure tricks*. You now have four diamonds, one spade, three hearts, and one club. In other words, you have nine sure tricks without having to do any more establishing, finessing, or giving up the lead. Therefore, when East returns a club, you should not try a risky and unnecessary finesse; you should rise with the ace of clubs and take your nine tricks.

Maybe you can see that *you should always try to take your finesse into the non-danger hand*. In that way, if the finesses lose, you are still safe.

Notice that if you had taken the club finesse, you would not have made your contract. West would have taken the king of clubs and his two remaining spade tricks to defeat you easily.

Now let's take a look at the other case—the case in which the danger hand could conceivably lead through one of your honor cards over to a higher honor in his partner's hand:

NORTH
♠ K Q 2
♡ 7
♢ A J 10 7 5 2
♣ Q J 2

WEST
♠ J 10 9 8 4
♡ A 8 4 3
♢ 6 4
♣ K 8

EAST
♠ 5 3
♡ Q J 10 9 6 2
♢ K 9 3
♣ 5 4

SOUTH
♠ A 7 6
♡ K 5
♢ Q 8
♣ A 10 9 7 6 3

Guess what the contract is? Right—3 NT. West leads the jack of spades and there you are. You have exactly five sure tricks, and your heart stopper is not exactly something to boast about.

You can establish either your clubs or your diamonds, and if you lose a trick in the suit you are establishing, you will have established enough sure tricks to make your contract.

Which suit should you establish? Take another look at your heart stopper. You don't know who has the ace of hearts, but you do know that if West has the ace, you do not want East *leading through your king;* therefore, East is the danger hand. And you always *take your finesses into the non-danger hand.*

The correct play is to win the spade lead in dummy and then lead the queen of clubs, playing low from your hand. West will play his king, and you are now completely safe. You have nine sure tricks—count them: five clubs, three spades, and a diamond. Even if West decides to shift to a heart, you must take a trick with the king, and then you can run off your sure tricks. What if West, after winning the club, decides to shift to a diamond? You should give him a disdainful look and play your ace. After all, you're no beginner. You are not about to take a finesse *into* the danger hand when you have enough sure tricks to make your contract. The nerve that he would even think that you might make a mistake!

Let's see what you've learned about the danger hand.

(a)

NORTH
♠ A J 10 9
♡ Q 4 3
◊ 7 5
♣ A J 10 9

SOUTH
♠ Q 4
♡ A J 10 9
◊ A 9 6
♣ K Q 8 7

Contract: 3 NT
Opening lead: King of diamonds (West has bid diamonds.)

(a)   How many sure tricks do you have?
(b)   Which diamond are you planning to take?
(c)   Who do you think is the danger hand, and which
        suit are you going to attack first?

(b)   NORTH
                    ♠ 4 3
                    ♡ A 7 6
                    ◊ A K J 7 6
                    ♣ 10 9 8

                    SOUTH
                    ♠ K 7
                    ♡ K Q 2
                    ◊ 10 9 8
                    ♣ A K J 7 6

Contract: 3 NT
Opening lead: Jack of hearts

(a)   How many sure tricks do you have?
(b)   Who is the danger hand? Why?
(c)   Which suit should you plan to establish?

Solutions

(a)   NORTH
                    ♠ A J 10 9
                    ♡ Q 4 3
                    ◊ 7 5
                    ♣ A J 10 9

WEST   EAST
♠ 8 7 6   ♠ K 5 3 2
♡ K 5 2   ♡ 8 7 6
◊ K Q J 8 4   ◊ 10 3 2
♣ 3 2   ♣ 6 5 4

                    SOUTH
                    ♠ Q 4
                    ♡ A J 10 9
                    ◊ A 9 6
                    ♣ K Q 8 7

South should count seven sure tricks: four clubs and three aces. Because of the weakness in the diamond suit, South should plan to win the third round of diamonds with the ace. This should make West the danger hand, as East is probably out of diamonds at this point.

As the general rule is "always finesse into the non-danger hand," you should plan to establish spades by leading the queen and playing low from dummy. If East has the king, you will lose your finesse, but you will have established two additional spade tricks for yourself, which will bring your total to nine.

If East happens to return a heart, you should rise with the ace, since you have your nine tricks and there is no point in finessing into the danger hand when you have your contract assured.

Had you thought that East was the danger hand (had he bid diamonds), then your plan would have been to finesse the heart into the West hand and not touch the spade suit at all.

(b)

NORTH
♠ 4 3
♡ A 7 6
◇ A K J 7 6
♣ 10 9 8

WEST
♠ A 8 6 2
♡ J 10 9 8
◇ 3 2
♣ Q 5 4

EAST
♠ Q J 10 9 5
♡ 5 4 3
◇ Q 5 4
♣ 3 2

SOUTH
♠ K 7
♡ K Q 2
◇ 10 9 8
♣ A K J 7 6

Again you have exactly seven sure tricks: three hearts and the ace and king of both clubs and diamonds.

Here it is clear that East is the danger hand because of your spade weakness. You do not want to expose yourself to a spade attack from East. If West has the ace of spades and East gets in and leads a spade, the opponents will be taking spade tricks for the next half hour. The idea, therefore, is to keep East away from the lead.

Fortunately, you have a choice of two suits to develop, clubs and diamonds. You are missing the queen in each suit, and you can finesse for the queen either by leading the ten of clubs from dummy and playing low or by leading the ten of diamonds from your hand and playing low.

In the first case you would be finessing into West, the non-danger hand, and that would be your proper play. Notice that the finesse in clubs loses, but that if West shifts to a spade, you must make a trick with your king. Then you will be able to take all of your established clubs, actually making an overtrick. Notice also what would have happened to you had you finessed the diamond instead. East would have won and returned the queen of spades. End of you.

KEY POINTERS

(1)   When playing a notrump contract, the opponents have the disturbing habit of leading your weakest suit. If you happen to have the ace of this suit, it is usually wisest to hold up until the third round of the suit before taking the trick. This hold-up play usually results in one opponent's having good cards in that suit and his partner's not having any cards at all in that suit. In this case the player with the good cards is called the danger hand, and the player without is called the non-danger hand.

(2)   The declarer's objective is to try like the devil to prevent the danger hand from getting the lead. This is usually accomplished by taking all finesses (if possible) into the non-danger hand. *Always try to finesse into the non-danger hand.*

(3)   Another possibility declarer must consider is that of an opponent's leading through unprotected honor cards in either declarer's hand or dummy. The opponent who can lead through the honor is considered the danger hand, and declarer tries to avoid this rather unpleasant occurrence.

(4)   There will be many hands where both opponents are

"dangerous." This should never deter you from taking finesses or establishing tricks if you do not have enough sure tricks to make your contract.

(5)   On the other hand, if you do have enough tricks to make your contract, don't play the hero and take any unnecessary finesses into the danger hand.

Part II

TRUMP PLAY

♠ ♡ ◊ ♣

7

The Trump Suit

♠ ♡ ◇ ♣

What is the difference between playing a hand at notrump and playing it with a trump suit? Let's take a look at this deal:

                        NORTH
                        ♠ Q 8 5 3
                        ♡ 7 6 3
                        ◇ A K Q
                        ♣ A 7 5

    WEST   EAST
    ♠ 10 6   ♠ 7 4
    ♡ A K Q J 2   ♡ 10 9 5
    ◇ 8   ◇ J 10 7 5 4 3
    ♣ 10 9 6 3 2   ♣ J 8

                        SOUTH
                        ♠ A K J 9 2
                        ♡ 8 4
                        ◇ 9 6 2
                        ♣ K Q 4

Presume that South is the declarer and that the contract is three notrump. South has eleven sure tricks—five spades, three diamonds, and three clubs—but he can take only eight tricks because the opponents have the opening lead! West can lead hearts and take the first five tricks. In other words, it doesn't matter how many sure tricks you have. If in a notrump contract you have one suit as weak as—or weaker than—the hearts in the above hand, the opponents, by leading that suit, can easily take the first five or six tricks while you sit there helplessly. What is the solution?

The solution is not to play hands in notrump when you and your partner have one suit completely unprotected. Those are the hands that should be played with a trump suit.

Go back to our example hand and assume that spades are trump. West still has the lead and starts out by playing the king, ace, and queen of hearts. South only has two hearts and can *trump* (or *ruff*) the queen of hearts with the lowly deuce of spades and take the trick!

Let's follow the hand a little further. Having trumped the third heart trick with a small spade, South now has the lead. He must now consider this problem: if he can trump the opponents' aces and kings, they can return the favor and trump his aces and kings!

Take a look at the diamond suit. If South leads a diamond to the ace on the board and then plays the king, West by that time will be void in diamonds and will gleefully trump South's king with his six of spades. How can South stop this? By taking away the opponents' small trumps *before* he plays his diamonds and clubs. Once the opponents have no more trumps, South has removed their fangs and can play his good clubs and diamonds in peace, knowing that they cannot be trumped.

Removing the opponents' trumps is called *drawing trumps*. On many hands declarer must draw the opponents' trumps before playing his other good tricks, in order to protect them from being trumped.

On this deal the opponents started with four trumps. South knows this because he has nine trumps between his hand and the dummy.

When playing a hand at a trump contract, the declarer *must* know how many trumps the opponents have at any given moment, and when he goes about removing them, he must be sure that they are *all* removed if that is his objective.

A rather simple method for doing this is to realize that every time you lead a trump and each of the opponents follows suit, two of their trump cards will be removed.

For example, on this hand the opponents started with four trumps. South leads the ace and everyone follows, so two of their four trumps have been played. South then plays the king and everyone follows again. When South led the king, he knew that the opponents had *two trump cards remaining,* and when both opponents followed suit, he knew that he had removed all of their trump cards.

Perhaps you have developed or will develop an easier method for counting trumps. This one is simple because normally you only have to keep in mind a small figure—usually four or five—which represents number of trumps the opponents have originally, and subtract each time an opponent plays a trump.

Going back to the original deal, South actually does take eleven tricks once he has drawn trumps. His three diamonds and three clubs are good to go along with his five tricks in spades, and so the story has a happy ending . . . provided that South plays in spades rather than in notrump.

KEY POINTERS

(1)   For a number of possible reasons, many hands should be played in a suit contract rather than in notrump. (Your partner's bidding helps you decide this.)

(2)   If the bidding determines that the hand should be played in a suit contract, then that suit becomes trump for that one hand. The power of the trump suit is such that if any player is void (has no cards) in a suit that has been led, he may put a trump card on that trick and take the trick—provided that no other player has placed a higher trump on that trick.

(3)   Declarer frequently draws (removes) the opponents' trump cards as soon as possible to prevent them from using their small trump cards to advantage.

(4)   Declarer must always know how many trumps the opponents had originally, and if he draws trumps, he must know when they do not have any more. (It is usually disadvantageous

to declarer to play trumps when the opponents do not have any more.) *Therefore, the declarer must count trumps.*

    (5)   New terminology:

Trump or ruff: Place a trump card upon a trick.

Draw trumps: Remove the opponents' trump cards.

8

Counting Losers

♠ ♡ ◇ ♣

Now that you have been brainwashed to count your sure tricks whenever you are declarer at notrump, guess what? At a suit contract you count your losers! This may seem like a rather negative way of going about playing a hand, but actually it's quite easy and helps you considerably in the play. Let's practice:

EXAMPLE HAND I

```
                    NORTH
                    ♠ 8 6 3 2
                    ♡ 9 8 5
                    ◇ A 4 2
                    ♣ A K Q

    WEST                            EAST
    ♠ 10 9                          ♠ 7
    ♡ A K Q                         ♡ J 10 4 2
    ◇ J 9 8 7 5 3                   ◇ K Q
    ♣ 8 4                           ♣ J 10 9 5 3 2

                    SOUTH
                    ♠ A K Q J 5 4
                    ♡ 7 6 3
                    ◇ 10 6
                    ♣ 7 6
```

South is the declarer at a contract of 4 ♠
West leads the king of hearts.

Now before playing a card from the dummy (even though
you know you are going to play a low heart), you plan the play
by *counting your losers* one suit at a time *beginning with the
trump suit.*

In the trump suit, spades, you are solid. That means you
have *no losers*. As a matter of fact, you are very well heeled in
spades You have ten of them, leaving the opponents with only
three small ones, which you should not have any trouble removing.

But there's a little trouble in the heart suit. When counting
losers, you first look to see how many losers there are in the hand
with the most trump. This is very important! Otherwise you can
get completely mixed up in counting these losers. The hand with
the larger number of trump will be called the long hand, and the
hand with the smaller number of trump will be called the short
hand. The long hand will almost always be the declarer, but once
in a while dummy will have more trump than the declarer, in
which case the dummy will be the long hand.

In this case South is the long hand and has three losing
hearts. But before counting three losers you must always look to
see if the short hand can take care of any of those losers. In this
case North also has three heart losers, so you must count three
losers in hearts.

In diamonds the long hand, South, has two losers, but the
short hand, North, has the ace, which will take care of one of
South's losers. Therefore, you count only one loser in diamonds.

In clubs South has two losers, but North has three winners.
How nice! In cases like this you count one *extra winner* in clubs
and your mental box-score should look like this:

  ♠   Solid, the opponents have only three small
          spades
  ♡   Three losers
  ◊   One loser
  ♣   One extra winner

Whether you like it or not, this is what you have to do on every hand you play at a suit contract.

Your next move is to determine whether you have more losers than you can afford in order to make your contract. In a contract of 4 ♠ you need ten tricks, so you can afford only three losers. If you have more than you can afford, you must try to get rid of these losers, if possible. There are a number of ways to get rid of losers; this chapter will deal with one common method . . . throwing losers on extra winners.

Let's play this hand out and see how it works.

West leads his three top hearts and you are helpless to do anything but follow suit. So you have lost heart tricks, but *it was inevitable*. Certain losers are inevitable; you can do nothing to prevent losing those tricks. The obvious case is when the opponents lead high cards in a side suit and you must follow suit.

After taking the first three tricks in hearts, West leads the seven of diamonds. You should take this trick with the ace in dummy. Now you still have one little diamond—a loser. There is a strong temptation at this point to get rid of that loser as quickly as possible since it may be making you nervous to look at it.

Notice that you have the ace, king, and queen of clubs. You could play them and on the third club discard your losing diamond, couldn't you? But wait a minute. West only has two clubs; he would trump the third club with the nine of spades and thus defeat your contract. Do you see what you should do? First you should remove the opponents' trumps, and then you should play your extra winners.

After you play the ace of diamonds, you should play the ace and king of spades (meanwhile counting their trumps, I hope), and after you have drawn their trumps, you can play your ace, king, and queen of clubs and discard your losing diamond on the third round without worrying about someone trumping one of your good clubs.

After a hand like this bridge might look like an easy game. You count your losers, draw their trumps, and then use your extra winners. But wait. Let's take a look at this hand before you become too cocky.

EXAMPLE HAND II

NORTH
♠ 10 5 3 2
♡ K Q 4
◊ A 7 2
♣ K 8 3

WEST
♠ A 6
♡ J 9 8 3
◊ K Q J
♣ 9 7 5 4

EAST
♠ 7 4
♡ 10 7 6 2
◊ 10 6 4 3
♣ A 6 2

SOUTH
♠ K Q J 9 8
♡ A 5
◊ 9 8 5
♣ Q J 10

Once again you, South, have become the declarer in a contract of 4 ♠ This time West leads the king of diamonds, and you take time out to count your losers, starting with the trump suit. Before reading any further, go ahead and count your losers, and we'll see if we come up with the same figure.

You should have counted one loser in spades; you must lose one trick to the ace. You have no losers in hearts; in fact, you have an extra winner. You have two losers in diamonds and one loser in clubs.

You have a total of four losers and one extra winner, or three losers once you use your extra winner.

Now on the first hand we drew trumps and then threw away one of our losers on one of our extra winners. *But this hand is different!*

Let's say we win the first trick with the ace of diamonds and then begin to draw trumps. We are missing the ace, and that means we must give up the lead. What can happen if we give up the lead? After playing the ace of trumps, West will take his two tricks in diamonds. Eventually we must lose a club to East's ace, and our contract will then be defeated.

What happened? What happened was that we never got to use our extra winner in hearts. It's still there! We drew trumps too quickly. By playing trumps before hearts, we allowed the opponents the advantage of getting the lead, after which they naturally took their two diamond tricks.

In order to make this hand, we must get rid of one of our diamonds *before* the opponents regain the lead to take their two diamond tricks. In other words, we must play hearts immediately —before drawing trumps! Our diamond losers are "immediate," which means we must get rid of them *before* the opponents regain the lead.

The proper play is to win the first trick with the ace of diamonds, then lead a low heart to the ace (high card from the short side), then lead a low heart back to the queen, and then play the king of hearts, discarding a diamond from your hand.

You are probably thinking that it is rather dangerous to play three rounds of hearts before drawing trumps. The answer is: *you have no choice.* If you let the opponents get the lead, you will automatically be defeated in your contract. You must take a small risk by playing three rounds of hearts before playing trumps. (The odds, however, are on your side: the opponents did start with eight hearts, and it is unlikely that one opponent has fewer than three hearts.) But you must see that you are playing give-up bridge if you lead trumps before hearts.

What are the factors which enable us to determine whether we should draw trumps first and then play our extra winners, or play the extra winners first? There are a few:

THE CONTRACT

> If you can make your contract by drawing trumps before playing your extra winners, you should do so. If you cannot make your contract without using your extra winners, you must decide whether to use your extra winners before or after drawing trumps. This depends upon the solidity of the trump suit.

THE TRUMP SUIT

> If the trump suit is solid (has no losers), declarer can draw trumps before playing his extra winners.

If the trump suit is not solid, then the important factor is the immediacy of the losers.

THE IMMEDIATE LOSERS

If the losers are immediate (that is, if the defense can take them the moment they regain the lead), then the declarer must risk playing his extra winners before allowing the opponents to regain the lead—in other words, before playing trumps if there is a trump loser.

THE EVENTUAL LOSERS

If the losers are eventual (A x x facing K x x, for instance), the declarer need not worry about using his extra winners until his eventual losers become immediate ones. With no immediate losers, declarer can draw trumps regardless of the solidity of the trump suit as he need not fear giving up the lead.

Example Hand II should give you a good idea of the difference between immediate and eventual losers if you will simply glance at the diamond suit. There are two losers in diamonds. If the opponents lead a diamond and we take it with the ace, our losers in diamonds are immediate; the ace having been removed, our opponents could take them immediately upon getting the lead. However, if the opponents lead another suit, our diamond losers are eventual; if the opponents got the lead, they could not take their diamond tricks until they knocked out our ace. That is why with a diamond lead we must use our extra winners before drawing trumps and surrendering the lead to the ace. But if a heart were led, we would have time to draw trumps before discarding our diamond loser on the heart in dummy.

The five problems which follow will give you a chance to count your losers and extra winners and to decide whether to use your extra winners before or after drawing trumps—or perhaps not at all.

Before you decide, check your contract. You may not need to risk using your extra winners. Risking your contract by playing extra winners too soon is just as much a bonehead play as not using them at all when you need them desperately in order to make your contract.

(a)

NORTH
♠ K Q 2
♡ J 10 7 6 5 4
♦ 3
♣ A 7 6

SOUTH
♠ A 5
♡ 3
♦ K Q J 10 8 7 6 5
♣ 9 4

The contract it 5 ♦ and the lead is the jack of clubs.
(a) How many losers do you have?
(b) Do you have any extra winners?
(c) What is your plan? (Do you draw trumps first or not?)

(b)

NORTH
♠ A 6 5
♡ Q 10 6 5
♦ Q J 10
♣ A Q 6

SOUTH
♠ 7 3 2
♡ A K J 9 7 4
♦ 8 4
♣ K 9

The contract is 4 ♡ and the opening lead is the queen of spades.
(a) How many losers do you have?
(b) Do you have any extra winners?

(c)   What is your plan? (Do you draw trumps first or
      not?)

(c)   NORTH
                        ♠ A K Q 7 6 5
                        ♡ K 6
                        ◊ A 6
                        ♣ K 7 6

                        SOUTH
                        ♠ J 8 4
                        ♡ Q J 10 9 8 7
                        ◊ 9 5
                        ♣ Q 2

The contract is 4 ♡ and the opening lead is the king of
diamonds.
(a)   How many losers do you have?
(b)   Do you have any extra winners?
(c)   What is your plan? (Do you draw trumps first or not?)

(d)   NORTH
                        ♠ K 5 4
                        ♡ Q J 10
                        ◊ A K Q 4 3
                        ♣ 7 6

                        SOUTH
                        ♠ A 8 3
                        ♡ 9 8 7 6 5 2
                        ◊ 7 2
                        ♣ K 5

The contract is 4 ♡ and the lead is the queen of clubs.
East, on your right, takes with the ace and returns a club.
You take with the king.
(a)   How many losers do you have?
(b)   Do you have any extra winners?
(c)   What is your plan? (Do you draw trumps first or not?)

(e)

NORTH
♠ K J 10 3
♡ 6 5 4
◇ A K Q 2
♣ 7 6

SOUTH
♠ Q 9 8 7 6 4
♡ A 7 3
◇ 9 4
♣ K 5

The contract is 3 ♠ and West leads the queen of clubs.
East takes the ace and returns the queen of hearts.
And you take that with your ace.
(a)   How many losers do you have?
(b)   Do you have any extra winners?
(c)   What is your plan? (Do you draw trumps first or not?)

Solutions

(a)   You have three losers—one in trumps, one in hearts,
       and one in clubs. However, as a saving grace, you
       have one extra winner in spades. Because your losers
       are *immediate* and because you do not have trump
       control, you must discard either your club loser or
       your heart loser on the queen of spades *before draw-
       ing trumps*. The correct play is to take the first trick
       with the ace of clubs, then play a spade to the ace,
       then lead a spade back to the king, and then discard
       a loser on the queen of spades. After that you should
       immediately lead a trump and force out the ace. In
       the end you will lose only two tricks and will make
       your contract.
(b)   This time you have four losers—two in spades and
       two in diamonds. Your plan should be to take the
       first trick with the ace of spades, remove the oppo-
       nents' trump cards (this time *you* have trump con-
       trol), and then play the king of clubs (high card from

the short side), then a club to dummy's queen, and then the ace, discarding a spade (or a diamond) from your hand. You wind up losing three tricks and making your contract.

(c) Be careful! You have three losers—one in hearts, one in clubs, and one in diamonds—and you have three extra winners in spades. But . . . there are two reasons why you should begin to draw trumps immediately after winning the diamond lead. In the first place, you can afford three losers and still make your contract; secondly, the extra winners in spades are too dangerous to take. *You have too many spades.* Therefore, one of your opponents must be short in spades. You will be risking your contract needlessly if you play spades before trumps. After taking the first trick, your proper play is the king of hearts.

(d) This time you have four losers—the ace of clubs (which the opponents have already played), the ace and king of trumps, and a spade. To compensate, you have one extra winner in diamonds. However, there is no hurry to discard your spade loser on the diamond, since you still have spade control. Your spade loser is eventual, which means you have time. You should lead a trump at trick two. Assume one opponent wins and leads a spade. You play the ace and then lead another trump. Let's assume this loses and another spade is led. You win this with the king and then draw any remaining trump. And then you discard your losing spade on the good queen of diamonds. This is a perfect example of the case in which, having eventual losers, you should save your extra winners until after you draw trumps.

(e) Be careful! This time you are in a contract of 3 ♠ which means that you can afford four losers and still make your contract. You have one loser in trumps, two in hearts, and one in clubs. That makes a total of four losers, and you have an extra winner in diamonds. Should you use your extra winner before letting the opponents in with the ace of trumps? The answer is *no*. There is no need to jeopardize a safe contract by playing your diamonds and risking a ruff. Making an extra trick is not nearly as important as insuring your contract. You should play a trump at trick two and let the opponents take their four tricks.

However, if you were to play the same hand in a contract of 4 ♠ then you would have to risk playing three high diamonds before drawing trumps, since that would be the only way to make your contract. *The same hand may easily be played in two different ways, depending upon the contract.*

KEY POINTERS

(1)   At a suit contract declarer counts his losers; at no-trump, his sure tricks.

(2)   When counting losers, count them from the *long hand*. The long hand is the hand which originally had more trumps—it is usually the declarer's hand.

(3)   Declarer must always relate the number of losers he counts to his contract. If he has more than he can afford, he must begin to look for a parking place for these losers. If he does not, he can relax.

(4)   There are two types of losers—immediate and eventual.

(5)   An immediate loser is one which the defense can take immediately upon getting the lead.

(6)   An eventual loser is a loser which cannot be taken by the defense immediately upon getting the lead (because declarer or dummy has control of the suit—by holding the ace, for instance).

(7)   To counterbalance losers, declarer may have *extra winners*.

(8)   An extra winner in a suit means that in that suit declarer not only has no loser but also has an additional good trick, upon which, when he plays it, he can discard a loser in another suit.

(9)   Declarer's primary concern is with his immediate losers. If he has more losers than he can afford in order to make his contract, then he must try to discard his immediate losers on his extra winners.

(10)   The problem of whether to draw trumps before using the extra winners depends upon the immediacy of the losers and the strength of the trump suit.

(11)   If the losers are of the immediate variety and declarer has more than he can afford, he draws trumps first—*provided that his trumps are solid* (see problem (b))—and then uses his extra winners. If his trumps have a loser, then he must use his extra winners before drawing trumps (see problem (a)).

(12)   If declarer's losers are eventual, he can draw trumps first and then discard his losers on his extra winners (see problem (d)).

(13)   Playing extra winners before drawing trumps demands a certain amount of courage from the declarer because there is always the possibility that one of the extra winners will be trumped. Declarer must keep in mind, however, that the only reason he is playing his extra winners before drawing trumps is that he cannot afford to give up the lead in trumps; he has too many losers to make his contract if he does not play his extra winners immediately. In other words, it is better to at least try to make the contract by playing extra winners than to give up without a struggle.

(14)   This has been said before but it is so important that it bears repeating. *There is no need to get rid of your losers on extra winners before drawing trumps if you do not have more losers than you can afford. Therefore, you must know on each hand how many losers you can afford in order to make your contract and whether you are taking unnecessary risks or mandatory ones.*

NORTH
♠ A 3 2
♡ 6 5
◊ A K Q 5 2
♣ 4 3 2

SOUTH
♠ 6 5 4
♡ K Q J 10 9 8
◊ 4 3
♣ A K

Consider this hand; it is the key to this chapter. Let's assume you are in a contract of 4 ♡ and West leads the king of spades. You count two losers in spades, one in trumps, and none in clubs or diamonds. As a matter of fact, you have an extra winner in diamonds. *But you don't really need that extra winner in diamonds, because you can afford to lose three tricks and still make 4 ♡ So you abandon your extra winner in diamonds because you would risk your safe contract if you played diamonds now. Someone might trump the second diamond, and you would wind up losing four tricks instead of three, in which case you would have created an extra loser for yourself for no reason.*

Now let's take the same hand and pretend the contract is 5 ♡ with the same opening lead. We have the same losers and the same extra winner, but this time we must use our extra winner *before* playing trumps *because we have more losers than we can afford.* In a contract of 5 ♡ we can afford only two losers in order to make the hand. Therefore, it is imperative that we discard our spade loser *before* giving up the lead. This time if our diamond is trumped, we will have created an extra loser for ourselves, but it won't have cost us our contract. We will simply be defeated by one extra trick, *which is meaningless.* We will have risked practically nothing *to try to make our contract,* which is all-important. Which leads us to this conclusion: the same hand played at different levels often has to be played differently. *It all depends upon the number of losers you can afford.*

9

Creating Extra Winners

♠ ♡ ◇ ♣

Life would be pretty grim if it weren't for extra winners. And an alert player is always on the lookout for them. They come in several forms. Until now we have dealt with immediate extra winners, extra winners which are ready-made. They take no work on our part at all. For example:

NORTH

♠ A K Q

SOUTH

♠ 4 3

ESTABLISHING EXTRA WINNERS BY FORCE

If another suit were trump, we would cheerfully count one immediate extra winner for ourselves in spades. However, in real life we are not always so fortunate. We usually have something that looks like this:

NORTH

♠ K Q J

SOUTH

♠ 4 3

In a side suit like this, we would count one loser, but we should realize that if we knock out the ace, we could create an extra winner for ourselves—a process similar to establishing extra tricks at notrump.

Now take a look at this one:

NORTH

♠ Q J 10

SOUTH

♠ 9 2

With what we have learned so far, it is easy to see that this suit offers not only two losers but also the possibility of creating an extra winner if we have time. We would have to lead the suit twice and hope that we could establish one winner before the opponents could take a trick in a suit in which we had an eventual loser. So it's somewhat like a race.

EXAMPLE HAND I

NORTH
♠ Q J 10
♡ A 3 2
◇ K 10 7 6
♣ 6 5 4

WEST   EAST
♠ A 8 7   ♠ K 6 5 4 3
♡ Q J 10 9   ♡ 8 7 6
◇ 3 2   ◇ 4
♣ Q J 10 9   ♣ 8 7 3 2

SOUTH
♠ 3 2
♡ K 5 4
◇ A Q J 9 8 5
♣ A K

The contract is 5 ◇ and West leads the queen of clubs. We count our losers—two in spades and one in hearts. We have no immediate extra winners, but we can create an extra winner in spades by giving up two tricks in the suit and making our third spade good.

We should win the club lead, draw two rounds of trumps, and then lead a spade. For the sake of argument, let's say that East takes the spade lead with the king and finds our weak spot, hearts. We win the heart return with our king and lead a second spade to West's ace. West returns a heart, knocking out our ace and leaving us with an immediate heart loser. But no matter —we have established or created an extra winner in spades, and we can now discard our losing heart on dummy's good spade. We wind up making our contract of 5 ♦ but it was a struggle.

We can learn quite a bit from this deal, so let's go back. Did you notice that West led the queen of clubs? What do you think would have happened if West had led the queen of hearts?

We would have taken the trick, drawn trumps, and led a spade. East would have won the spade, as before, and returned a heart. We would have won the heart in dummy and played a spade, establishing an extra winner for ourselves. But West would have had the last laugh: he would have won the spade trick and taken the setting trick in hearts. Even though our spade was good in dummy, we would not have had the *time* to use it.

In fact, there is nothing we could have done against a heart lead. The hand cannot be made if West leads a heart. Maybe now you can see how important it is for the defense to choose the proper suit to lead. Sometimes it is no more than a guess. So you see that the element of chance is now rearing its ugly head.

The time has come to discuss the difference between suits which are evenly divided (have the same number of cards) between declarer and dummy and those which are unevenly divided (either declarer or dummy having more cards in the suit). For example:

NORTH

♠ A 3 2

SOUTH

♠ K 5 4

In this case both declarer and dummy have the same number

of cards. This is a one-loser suit, and that loser is an eventual loser. The opponents would have to lead the suit twice before it would become an immediate loser. But that is not the point. *Whenever declarer and dummy have the same number of cards in a side suit, it is impossible to create an extra winner in that suit.*

An equal number of cards in the two hands is death to the declarer. He cannot work with that kind of suit. He must work with suits which are unequally divided between the two hands. Consider this side suit:

NORTH

♠ K Q 4

WEST   EAST

♠ 9 8 7 6   ♠ A 10 5 3

SOUTH

♠ J 2

Let's say that you are South and wish to create an extra winner for yourself. This spade suit offers an excellent prospect. You lead the jack (high card from the short side), and let's assume that East wins the trick with the ace. You now have created an extra winner. It was that easy. But what if East does not take the jack but takes the second round of the suit instead? In that case, this is what your spade suit would look like:

NORTH

♠ K

WEST   EAST

♠ 9 8   ♠ 10 5

SOUTH

You would have an extra spade winner in dummy, but it would do you no good if you had no way of getting over to the dummy in order to use it. You can learn two facts from this example:

(1)   *In order to create extra winners, you must play suits which are unevenly divided between your hand and the dummy.*

(2)   *It does you no good to create extra winners if you have no way of using them. Therefore, you must save an entry in another suit to be able to use the extra winners you have created.*

Let's see another example of this:

EXAMPLE HAND II

```
                    NORTH
                    ♠ 5 4 3 2
                    ♡ 7 6 5
                    ◇ A 5 4
                    ♣ K Q 2

     WEST                          EAST
     ♠ 9                           ♠ 10
     ♡ K J 3 2                     ♡ Q 10 9 8
     ◇ Q J 9 8                     ◇ 10 7 6 3
     ♣ 9 8 7 6                     ♣ A 10 5 4

                    SOUTH
                    ♠ A K Q J 8 7 6
                    ♡ A 4
                    ◇ K 2
                    ♣ J 3
```

South's contract is 6 ♠ and West leads the queen of diamonds. South counts two losers—one in hearts (eventual) and one in clubs. However, after he loses his trick in clubs, he has created an extra winner in that suit.

South's plan should be to establish a club discard for his losing heart. But where should South take the first trick? In his hand or in the dummy?

South *must* win the first diamond in his hand with the king *in order to save a later entry to the dummy with the ace of diamonds*. Remember, our plan is to play the jack of clubs and drive out the ace. Then we will have a small club with which to get to dummy. But what if they don't take the jack but instead take the next one? Then how will we get to dummy? That's why we win the opening lead with the king of diamonds, retaining the ace for a *later entry* to our established club trick.

After winning the opening lead, we play the ace of spades, which draws all of the opponents' trumps. Now the jack of clubs, followed by another club if the jack is ducked. (If the opponents duck two rounds of clubs, we make our contract by not losing a club at all.) East wins the second club trick and returns a heart. We win the ace and enter dummy with the ace of diamonds to discard our losing heart on the high club.

Notice that this is another hand which could have been defeated with a different opening lead. A heart lead would have made South's heart loser immediate, and South would not have been able to use the club discard, as the opponents would have taken their heart trick upon gaining the lead with the ace of clubs.

CREATING EXTRA WINNERS BY FINESSING OR LEADING UP TO BROKEN STRENGTH

In the previous examples extra winners have been either there for the taking or establishable by force. Establishing by force simply means creating extra winners without finessing. You can lead the suit that you are establishing from either your hand or the dummy and get the same result.

Here are a few examples of establishing by force (note that there is an unequal number of cards on each side):

(1)   NORTH
       ♠ Q J 10
    SOUTH
       ♠ 3 2

(2)   NORTH
       ♠ K Q J
    SOUTH
       ♠ 3 2

(3)   NORTH
       ♠ K Q 2
    SOUTH
       ♠ J 3

(4)   NORTH
       ♠ Q J 3 2
    SOUTH
       ♠ K 4

In each of these four examples, declarer can establish one extra winner in the spade suit *by initiating the suit from either side*. In other words, in (1) it doesn't matter whether you lead the queen from the dummy or the two from your hand towards the queen in the dummy; the end result is the same. The same applies in (2). You can lead the king from dummy or a low one towards the king; it's all the same. In (3) you lead either the jack (high card from short side) or low towards the jack. In (4), either the king or low to the king.

Remember our friend, the finesse, from the notrump chapter? It is pertinent again in this pair of examples:

(1)

> NORTH
> ♠ A Q J
>
> WEST   EAST
> ?   ?
>
> SOUTH
> ♠ 4 3 2

(2)

> NORTH
> ♠ A Q J
>
> WEST   EAST
> ?   ?
>
> SOUTH
> ♠ 3 2

Assume that in each case you are dealing with a side suit at a suit contract. In (1) you should mentally think to yourself that if West has the king, you have no spade losers, but if East has the king, you have one spade loser. You may have no way of knowing who has the king, but you do know one thing: *you cannot create any extra winners in spades because you have the same number of spades in both your hand and the dummy*. You either have one loser or no loser in spades. Period.

Now let's look at (2). Again, you don't know where the king is. Assume temporarily that it is with West; this means that the finesse works. Remember, *when finessing you must lead from weakness towards broken strength.* So you lead the two and play the queen from dummy, and it takes the trick. You then come back to your hand and lead the three, and when West plays low, you finesse the jack. Assuming this wins, your ace is good, and you have created an extra winner.

Now let's assume you lead the two and finesse the queen but that this time East wins the king. What do you have left? You have the ace and jack in dummy and only the three in your hand. In other words, you have created an extra winner for yourself even though the finesse lost!

What conclusion can we reach? *When we have a choice of finesses to take and we wish to create extra winners, we should, if possible, take the finesse in the unevenly divided suit before taking the finesse in the evenly divided suit.*

Let's put those identical suits in a bridge hand and see how this works:

EXAMPLE HAND III

```
                        NORTH
                        ♠ A Q J
                        ♡ 7 5 3 2
                        ◇ A Q J
                        ♣ 7 6 5
        WEST                            EAST
        ♠ K 10 5 4                      ♠ 9 8 7 6
        ♡ 4                             ♡ 8 6
        ◇ 9 8 3 2                       ◇ K 10 7
        ♣ K Q 10 2                      ♣ J 9 8 4
                        SOUTH
                        ♠ 3 2
                        ♡ A K Q J 10 9
                        ◇ 6 5 4
                        ♣ A 3
```

South plays in 6 ♡ and West leads the king of clubs. South counts his losers—one possible loser in spades, one possible loser in diamonds, and one immediate loser in clubs. What to do? Obviously, South is going to have to take finesses in both diamonds and spades, but which one first? *The unevenly divided one.*

Souths wins the club, draws two rounds of trumps, and then leads a spade to the queen, which holds. He then comes back to his hand with a trump and leads another spade to the jack, which also holds. Then he plays the ace of spades and discards his losing club.

Things are looking up. South trumps a club to re-enter his hand and then leads a diamond to the queen. East takes the king, but that is the last defensive trick. South makes his small slam.

Now let's see what happens if South finesses diamonds before spades: East wins the king of diamonds and plays a club, and South is defeated by one trick. Quite a difference.

In case you are wondering what would have happened if the king of spades and the king of diamonds had been reversed, the answer is that you could not have made the hand! The contract depended upon the king of spades. The king of diamonds had nothing to do with this hand! It was a mirage! The king of spades is the decisive card; if East has it, the contract is defeated, and if West has it, the contract is made.

You might not believe this, but many players who have played for years would not know which finesse to take first. But you *will* know!

Remember, a finesse is not always leading up to an ace-queen combination in dummy. Here are a few other quite common finessing positions in unevenly divided suits (the suits you should be working on first):

(1)   NORTH
                            ♠ K 6 5 4

        WEST   EAST
          ?   ?

                            SOUTH
                            ♠ 3

South should lead the three from his hand towards the king. If West has the ace and takes the trick, then the king in dummy will be established as an extra winner. If East has the ace—well, at least you tried.

(2)

NORTH

♠ K Q 5

WEST   EAST

?   ?

SOUTH

♠ 3 2

South leads the two, West plays low, and the king or queen in dummy takes the trick. Now what? South must re-enter his hand to repeat the finesse.

Maybe you can see that whenever you have to lead up to strength twice, which is called taking a *repeatable finesse,* you must be sure to have an entry back to your hand. This is how the spades might have been:

NORTH

♠ K Q 5

WEST   EAST

♠ A J 10 9   ♠ 8 7 6 4

SOUTH

♠ 3 2

You lead low and West plays the nine. You take the trick with the king, but the lead is in the dummy. If you wish to take a trick with the queen, you must come back to your hand *in another suit* and lead up to the queen. West will usually take the second spade, and that will make your queen good, *providing you have an entry to dummy in another suit.* Hopefully, you will now begin to plan your entry situation before playing a hand.

Here is an illustration:

EXAMPLE HAND IV

NORTH
♠ 3
♡ K Q 5 4
◇ A 7 6 5 4
♣ 8 7 6

WEST
♠ 5 4
♡ A J 10 9
◇ J 9 8
♣ A K Q 10

EAST
♠ 7 6 2
♡ 8 7 6
◇ K Q 10
♣ J 9 5 4

SOUTH
♠ A K Q J 10 9 8
♡ 3 2
◇ 3 2
♣ 3 2

The contract is 4 ♠ and West starts out with three rounds of clubs, South trumping the third. Now let's see where we stand.

Our trumps are solid, but we have a heart loser and a diamond loser. We must try to create an extra winner. The heart suit looks hopeful. If West has the ace, we can lead up to the dummy. If West takes the ace immediately, that will make both our king and queen good, and we will be able to discard a diamond.

But just a minute. West may not be so friendly. He may not take the first heart. He may be stubborn and play his nine. Then we would win the king or queen and be forced to repeat the finesse by re-entering our hand.

Do we have any way of re-entering our hand? Yes, but only in trumps. Do you see what this means? It means that after trumping the third club, we cannot draw trumps, *because the trump suit is the only suit which will give us an entry back to our hand in order to repeat the heart finesse.*

We must lead a heart immediately. Let's say West plays

the nine. We take it with the king, and then we return to our
hand with a trump and draw the remaining trumps. Now a second heart is led, West plays the ace, and we have created an
extra winner in hearts. We also have the ace of diamonds for the
entry to our good heart.

What if East had had the ace of hearts? Then the hand
could not have been made. What if the defense had shifted to a
diamond after taking two rounds of clubs? Then the hand could
not have been made. Besides, we are playing in too tough a game
if they find that defense!

What if we had drawn trumps before leading a heart? If
West ducks the first heart, as he should, he defeats the contract,
as we have no way of leading up to the hearts for a second time.

Notice all the variables in this hand. First, you must assume
that West has the ace of hearts in order to make the hand. Second, you must assume that West might duck the first heart lead.
Third, you must prepare entries for both the winner you have
created and the repeatable finesse that you are likely to need.

FINESSING WITH NO LOSERS IN THE SUIT

Let's say you encounter this situation:

NORTH

♠ A Q

WEST   EAST

?   ?

SOUTH

♠ 2

West leads a spade. Should you play the ace or the queen?
If your answer is "I can't tell until I see the whole hand," you
are getting pretty smart.

It's obvious that South has no losers in spades if he simply
plays the ace. But it should also be obvious that if South is desperate for an extra winner, his best chance is to play the queen
and hope West has the king.

Let's put this combination into an entire hand and see if you can work it out:

EXAMPLE HAND V

NORTH
♠ A Q
♡ K 3 2
♢ 7 6 5 4
♣ A 5 4 3

WEST   EAST
?   ?

SOUTH
♠ 2
♡ A 5 4
♢ K Q J 10 9 8 3
♣ K 2

South plays in 6 ♢ and West leads a low spade. Should you finesse? *Yes.* You have a certain trump loser (the ace) and an eventual heart loser. What are you going to do with that heart loser? It won't disappear, you know.

Your best chance to get rid of the heart is to play the queen of spades on the first trick. If the finesse works, you can throw your heart on the ace of spades after drawing trumps. If the finesse loses, you won't have lost anything.

Do you see why? Your ace of spades is still good, and you can throw the heart away on the ace of spades, so you wind up with the same number of losers even if the finesse loses. If it works, you make your slam. Furthermore, all your misery is over in one second. Either the queen of spades takes the trick and you make the hand, or East plays the king and you don't make the hand.

When a finesse does not cost a trick even if it loses, it is called a *free finesse.* Declarer should always be on the lookout for free finesses.

Let's see if you think this next hand involves a free finesse or not:

EXAMPLE HAND VI

NORTH
♠ A Q 6 5
♡ 10 8
◇ A 6 5 4
♣ A Q 10

WEST   **EAST**
  ?   ?

SOUTH
♠ 4
♡ J 9
◇ K Q J 10 9 8 3
♣ K J 9

South plays in 5 ◇ and West leads a low spade. Should South finesse? Only if he wants an award for the most poorly played hand of the year.

South has two immediate heart losers and no other losers at all. If the spade finesse loses, the opponents can take their two heart tricks and defeat the contract. This wouldn't be a free finesse, it would be a madness finesse! South is sure of his contract if he simply plays the ace of spades.

But what if South were playing the same hand in a contract of 6 ◇ and a small spade were led? In this case he would finesse the queen in an effort to create an extra winner on which to discard one of his two sure heart losers. If the finesse lost, the defense would take their two heart tricks and defeat the contract an extra trick. But if the finesse won, South would make his slam contract.

In an undoubled contract declarer should always risk going down an extra trick or two in order to make his contract.

Declarer should never risk a sure contract by taking an unnecessary risk.

One of the sweetest things that can happen to you as declarer is to have the opponents lead a suit in which you are void and your dummy has honor cards. When this happens, you play one of the lower honor cards. If it is covered, you can trump, and if it is not, your honor card takes the trick, and you can discard a loser. Now let's look at this hand:

EXAMPLE HAND VII

NORTH
♠ A 3 2
♡ A Q 6 5
◇ 7 6 5
♣ Q J 10

SOUTH
♠ K Q J 10 9 8 7
♡ none
◇ A 10 2
♣ A 3 2

You are playing in 6 ♠ and West leads a low heart. Which heart should you play from the dummy?

We have two eventual diamond losers and one possible club loser (depending upon the location of the king). We hope East has the king but we don't know. To counterbalance our losers, we have one extra heart winner and a beautiful opportunity for a second.

We simply play the queen of hearts on the first trick. Either the queen will hold the trick and we will have created an extra heart winner, or the queen will be covered and we will trump. Our ace of hearts is still over there, so we will have lost nothing by taking a free finesse in hearts. We might even make our slam if we get lucky.

Be on the alert for free finesses when you are void in the suit which the opponent has led.

Be sure to answer all of the questions under each problem before going on to the next.

(1)   NORTH
                       ♠ A 3 2
                       ♡ K Q 2
                       ◊ 4 3 2
                       ♣ 6 5 4 3

                       SOUTH
                       ♠ K 5 4
                       ♡ 7 6
                       ◊ A K Q J 10 9 8
                       ♣ A

The contract is 6 ◊ and West leads the queen of spades.

(a) Where do you win the first trick? Why?
(b) Does this contract depend upon the location of any
     key card?
(c) If so, which card and who do you hope has it?
(d) Can you afford to draw trumps on this hand?

(2)   NORTH
                       ♠ A J 10
                       ♡ A J 10
                       ◊ 7 6 5 4
                       ♣ 4 3 2

                       SOUTH
                       ♠ Q 3
                       ♡ Q 5 4
                       ◊ A 2
                       ♣ A K Q J 9 8

The contract is 6 ♣ and the lead is the king of diamonds.

(a) Does this contract depend upon the location of one
     or more than one key card?
(b) Can you afford to draw trumps?
(c) Which suit should you attack first? Why?
(d) Which card should you play in the suit which you at-
     tack?

(3)

NORTH
♠ K 7 6 5
♡ K 7 6
◇ J 7 6
♣ J 7 6

SOUTH
♠ 3
♡ A 5 3
◇ A Q 10 9 5 3
♣ 10 9 8

The contract is 2 ◇ and West leads the king, queen, and a low club to East's ace. East returns the queen of hearts at trick four.

(a) Where should you win this trick? Why?
(b) Which are the key cards on this hand?
(c) Where do you hope they are placed?
(d) Should you draw trumps immediately?

(4)

NORTH
♠ 7 6 5
♡ K 7 6 5
◇ A 4 3
♣ Q J 2

SOUTH
♠ K Q J 10 4 3
♡ A 4
◇ K 5 2
♣ 5 4

The contract is 4 ♠ and West leads the queen of hearts.

(a) How many losers do you have?
(b) Where should you win the opening lead and what should you lead at trick two?

(5)

NORTH
♠ 6 5 4
♡ A K J 6 5
♦ 7 6
♣ Q J 10

SOUTH
♠ A 8 3
♡ 2
♦ Q J 10 9 5 4
♣ A K 2

This is a two-part problem:

Part I: Assume you are in a contract of 4 ♦ and West
         leads the king of spades.
         (a)   How many losers do you have?
         (b)   How many extra winners?
         (c)   What is your plan?
Part II: Now assume you are in a contract of 5 ♦ with
         the same lead. Will this affect your plan in any
         way? If so, how?

Solutions

(1)   (a)   You should win the opening lead in your own
             hand in order to preserve a later entry to a possi-
             ble extra winner in hearts.
       (b)   Yes.
       (c)   The ace of hearts, and you must hope West has
             that card.
       (d)   Yes, you can draw trumps and then lead a heart.
             If the queen or king wins in dummy, you can
             come back to your hand with a club and lead
             another heart. If West has the ace, you make the
             slam. If East has it, join the club.
(2)   (a)   One card, the king of spades.
       (b)   Yes.

(c) Spades. You must attack the unevenly divided side suit first in order to establish an extra winner for your diamond loser.

(d) You must lead the queen of spades (high card from short side) in order to retain the lead in your hand in case the queen wins the trick. If the spade finesse works, you can repeat the finesse by leading a low spade to your jack and then discarding a diamond on the ace of spades. You would now trump a diamond back to your hand and lead the queen of hearts. If West has the king also, you make an overtrick; if not, you simply make your contract. If East started with the king of spades, forget it. He will play his king and return a diamond. Down one.

(3) (a) You should win this trick in your own hand as you are planning to lead a spade to the king—and if West has the ace, you want the king of hearts as an entry to your extra winner in spades.

(b) The ace of spades and the king of diamonds.

(c) You hope that West has the ace of spades and that East has the king of diamonds.

(d) No, you must first lead a spade to the king. If this loses to the ace in the East hand, then you must simply finesse the diamond to make the contract by leading the jack from dummy. However, if West has the ace of spades, you will have established an extra winner for your losing heart and will be able to make your contract regardless of the location of the king of diamonds.

(4) (a) You have four losers—one in trumps, two in clubs (immediate), and one in diamonds (eventual).

(b) You must create an extra winner in clubs before the opponents can establish their diamond trick. You should, therefore, lead a club immediately. Assuming this loses and a diamond comes back, you must win this in your own hand and play a second club. If the ace and king of clubs are divided, you will have established an extra winner in clubs *before* the opponents have established their diamond trick.

If you waste a tempo (let the opponents have the lead) by leading a trump, the opponents could defeat the contract by attacking diamonds before you can set up your club winner.

(5)   Part I:
   (a)   You have four losers.
   (b)   You have one sure extra winner in hearts.
   (c)   Your plan should be to win the spade and play the ace and king of hearts immediately, discarding one spade. Then you should draw trumps.

Part II:
   Now you must get rid of two of your losers before drawing trumps in order to make your contract. In a contract of 5 ♦ you have only one chance. You must lead a low heart at trick two and finesse the jack. You must try for two extra winners, and this is the only way. If West has the queen of hearts, you will be able to discard both of your spades on the ace and king of hearts. If East has the queen of hearts, you will go down three tricks instead of one, but it is still worth the gamble.

   The point of the problem is that you must create an additional extra winner in a contract of five diamonds by taking an unusual finesse. In 4 ♦ you did not have to take that risk.

KEY POINTERS

   (1)   Declarer must always be on the lookout for extra winners.
   (2)   These come in various forms. There are the immediate extra winners, those which can be taken without giving up the lead. There are extra winners which can be established by

knocking out high cards in the suit. Finally, there are extra winners which can be created by finessing.

(3)   One thing is common to all suits which are even being considered for extra winners. The cards in that suit must be unequally divided between declarer's hand and dummy's.

(4)   Declarer should normally postpone playing short suits which are equally divided between his hand and the dummy's (two opposite two or three opposite three). Those are usually the suits which have the eventual losers.

(5)   When creating extra winners, declarer must always be careful to retain a side entry to the suit which he is establishing. This entry may be either in trumps or in a side suit.

(6)   When finessing, always lead from weakness towards strength.

(7)   If this process must be repeated in the same suit, it is called a *repeatable finesse*. Declarer must always take care to preserve entries in order to be able to repeat finesses.

(8)   A *free finesse* is a finesse which, if it loses, does not cost declarer a trick because he will be able to discard one or more side losers whether the finesse works or not. An excellent example of this occurs when declarer has the ace-queen of a side suit in the dummy and a void of that suit in his hand. Assuming the suit is led from his left through the ace-queen, he should normally finesse the queen. If the king covers, he can trump and still use the ace later. If the queen wins, he has two discards.

(9)   If declarer needs a specific card in a specific opponent's hand in order to make a contract, he should assume that it is there and play accordingly.

(10)   Declarer should risk going down an extra trick or two to make his contract, providing he is not doubled.

10

Long Suit Establishment

♠   ♡   ◇   ♣

We have yet to discuss the main method of creating extra winners. Fortunately, we have already discussed long suit establishment at notrump, so this will simply be an extension. Let's go back to notrump and take a look at this combination:

NORTH
♠ A K 4 3 2

WEST
♠ 9 8 7

EAST
♠ Q J 10

SOUTH
♠ 6 5

We said that if South wishes to establish the smaller spades at notrump, he can play the ace, the king, and a low one, which will exhaust the opponents' spades and make the remaining two spades in dummy high. We also said that if there was no re-entry to dummy, it would be better to play a low spade from both hands and then play the ace and king, ending up in dummy with the good spades. In either case South makes four spade tricks but must concede one.

Now let's put that very same spade combination in a complete bridge hand, but this time hearts are trump:

NORTH
♠ A K 4 3 2
♡ A 9 3
◇ Q 3
♣ 9 5 4

WEST
♠ 9 8 7
♡ 4
◇ A K 6 5 2
♣ Q J 10 6

EAST
♠ Q J 10
♡ 7 6 5
◇ 10 9 7 4
♣ K 7 2

SOUTH
♠ 6 5
♡ K Q J 10 8 2
◇ J 8
♣ A 8 3

South is playing a contract of 4 ♡ and West starts out by taking the first two diamonds; he then leads the queen of clubs.

South has lost two tricks and after winning the ace of clubs, has two immediate club losers. South must start searching for extra winners—quickly!

The only possibility is the spade suit. In spades South has no losers, but no apparent extra winners either. Let's say that South plays the ace of spades and then the king of spades; he then leads a low spade from dummy and trumps it with the ten of hearts. All of the opponents' spades have fallen, and there are now two good spades in dummy! Two extra winners.

But how does South use them? *Extra winners are worthless if the opponents can trump them.* Therefore, South must draw trumps—*in this case ending where the extra winners are, because dummy has no side entries.* It would do South no good to draw three rounds of trumps and end up in his hand when the good spades are in dummy. His plan should be to play the king, the queen and then the ace; that will exhaust the opponents' trumps and allow him to use his two good spades to discard his two losing clubs.

Now you probably have some questions about this little

process of long suit establishment. They might be: What if the opponents' spades did not divide 3-3? Do I draw trumps before or after I establish my long suit? What if someone trumped either my ace or my king of spades? What if my trumps were not so strong and when I trumped a spade, my left-hand opponent overtrumped? How long must a suit be in order to establish it?

Before answering these questions, a few common-sense tips will help:

(1) It does no good to establish a long suit if you have no way of using the cards which you have established. In other words, you always need an entry to the suit which you have established.

(2) You need not risk establishing a long suit if you do not have more losers than you can afford in order to make your contract.

(3) If you have more losers than you can afford to make your contract, any risk within reason is worthwhile in order to establish a long suit.

Now let's go back to the questions:

What if the spades did not divide 3-3? It is true that the long suit you are developing may not always set up after trumping once. But there is no law against trumping twice! This is the same hand except for the fact that the spades are divided 4-2:

NORTH
♠ A K 4 3 2
♡ A 9 3
♢ Q 3
♣ 9 5 4

WEST
♠ 8 7
♡ 4
♢ A K 6 5 4 2
♣ Q J 10 6

EAST
♠ Q J 10 9
♡ 7 6 5
♢ 10 9 7
♣ K 7 2

SOUTH
♠ 6 5
♡ K Q J 10 8 2
♢ J 8
♣ A 8 3

Once again, the contract is 4 ♡ and West takes two diamond tricks and then leads the queen of clubs.

You see that you must establish your spades and that your only re-entries to dummy are in the trump suit, so you must save your entries until the spades are established. (This statement answers the question of whether you should draw trumps first. Not if the trumps are the sole entries!)

You play the ace and the king of spades and then trump a spade with the ten of hearts (choosing the ten to avoid being overtrumped if the spades are divided 4-2). And sure enough, West discards a diamond. You still have two little spades in dummy, but East has one higher spade.

So you lead your two of hearts to dummy's nine and then lead another spade and trump it with the eight. At this point your little spade in the dummy has been established. However, you cannot use it until you draw the opponents' remaining trumps.

You should know that they have two small trumps left. So you lead your king of hearts and then another heart to dummy's ace, drawing all of the trumps. Now you can play your good spade and discard one losing club to make your contract.

I'm sure you have noticed by now that when you are establishing dummy's long suit *you must count that suit to know when the small cards in dummy are good*. Most partners don't appreciate the humor in your continuing to trump small cards when the opponents don't have any more. *You must also count trumps because you must remove all of their trumps before using your established suit.*

Another important point: When spades divided 3-3, you needed only one dummy entry, the ace of hearts, in order to establish and use the spade suit. But when spades divided 4-2, then you needed both the nine and the ace in dummy as entries. This means that sometimes the dummy will not have sufficient entries for you to be able to establish your long suit, but if it does, you must make allowances for a possible uneven break and save as many entries to dummy as possible.

What if someone had trumped either the ace or the king of spades? If this happens, it means that the original spade division was 5-1, which is very unikely, but it also means that *you never could have made the hand in the first place*. If the spades were that badly bunched, you were doomed from the start, and by having one of your spades trumped, you only lost an extra trick which, as we said before, means nothing. *It pays to go down an extra trick or two to try to make your contract.*

What if your trumps weren't so strong and when you trumped, either the first or second spade, West, on your left, had overtrumped? The French have an expression for this—*c'est la vie*. If it happens, it happens, but before you trump with a low card, you must be sure that you can't spare a higher one. Look at the example hands. South did not trump the spade with the deuce; since his trumps were good enough for him to be able to trump high, he did not have to risk being overtrumped. However, there will be times when you will be forced to trump low, and then you must simply pray that you will not be overtrumped.

Of course, we are assuming that you could not draw trumps in the first place. When you set up a suit in dummy, you don't always have to leave the opponents' trumps at large. *It depends upon the entry situation.* Take a look at this hand:

```
                    NORTH
                    ♠ A K 4 3 2
                    ♡ 3 2
                    ◇ A 3 2
                    ♣ A 3 2

    WEST                            EAST
    ♠ 8 7                           ♠ Q J 10 9
    ♡ J 9 8                         ♡ 7 6
    ◇ Q J 10 9                      ◇ 8 7 6
    ♣ J 9 8 7                       ♣ Q 10 6 5

                    SOUTH
                    ♠ 6 5
                    ♡ A K Q 10 5 4
                    ◇ K 5 4
                    ♣ K 4
```

South plays in a contract of 7 ♡ and West leads the queen of diamonds. South counts one loser in diamonds and plans to establish the spade suit.

This time there are no trump entries to dummy, but there are two side entries, the minor-suit aces. Therefore, South can draw trumps before establishing the spade suit, but he must be careful *to win the first diamond trick in his hand in order to save entries to the hand of the side suit which he is establishing.*

South wins the first trick with the king of diamonds and then plays three rounds of trumps, discarding a diamond from the dummy. *Notice that you would never discard the suit that you are planning to establish.*

Then South plays the ace and the king and then trumps a spade, noticing that the suit did not divide 3-3. He re-enters dummy with the ace of diamonds (or clubs) and trumps another spade. Then he re-enters dummy with his remaining ace and discards his losing diamond on his established spade.

Had South started to establish spades before drawing trumps, West would have overtrumped and the contract would have been defeated.

It might help to digress a moment and show you how to count the suit you are establishing so that you don't pull a bonehead play by trumping a good trick. Let's look at this spade suit from the declarer's point of view:

NORTH

♠ A K 4 3 2

SOUTH

♠ 6 5

After you play the ace and king (assuming everyone follows), eight spades will have been played. You remain with three in the dummy, which means that there are two spades outstanding. You lead a low spade. If each opponent follows, there are no more spades outstanding; if one opponent shows out (has no more), you must trump still another spade to establish the suit. This method is called *counting by fours.*

Another way to count the spades is to ask yourself how many spades your opponents had originally. In this case, the answer is six. After you play the ace, they have four, and after you play the king, they have two. Use whichever method is easier for you—but you must count that suit!

(If you think you are having trouble counting, rest assured you are not alone. I have a friend who devised his own system. It goes like this: When the dummy is laid down, he sees how many spades he has between his hand and the dummy. Say he has six; that means the opponents have seven. Therefore, the first number he remembers is seven. He does the same thing in all four suits and winds up with something like this: 7586. This he calls his first telephone number. Now let's say a club is led, which means that the opponents each play a club; that changes the telephone number to 7584. In other words, after each trick he would have a new telephone number, which represents the number of cards the opponents hold in each suit. After hearing this explanation, I finally asked how this system actually worked in practice. He answered, "It's a great system, but I can never remember those - - - - telephone numbers.")

Now for the final question: How long must a suit be in order to establish it? Let's start with the ridiculous:

NORTH

♠ 6 5 4 3 2

WEST   **EAST**

♠ A J 10 9   ♠ K Q 8 7

SOUTH

♠ none

Assume that hearts are trumps and that South needs to establish an extra winner. Can he do so with that absolutely anemic spade suit? Yes! If South can get over to the dummy four times and trump a spade each time, and if the opponents' spades divide 4-4, and if South can get over to the dummy a fifth time to use the little spade he has established, it *can* be done!

Granted this is an *extreme* example: South would need enough trumps to trump four times in his own hand plus draw the opponents' trumps, and he would also need five side entries to dummy. But *it can be done.*

Therefore we can conclude: *any five-card suit can conceivably be established for at least one extra winner, given sufficient entries and trump strength.*

Fortunately, we normally don't have to work this hard. Let's go back to one of our more familiar combinations:

NORTH
♠ K Q 2

WEST   EAST
♠ A J 10 9   ♠ 8 7 6 5

SOUTH
♠ 4 3

Remember, we said that if you needed one extra winner from this suit, you would lead up to your king-queen twice; if West had the ace, you could make two tricks. If East had the ace, at least you tried.

Let's lengthen that suit a bit:

NORTH
♠ K Q 4 3 2

WEST   EAST
♠ A J 10   ♠ 9 8 7

SOUTH
♠ 6 5

Now instead of one extra winner, you can get three! You lead up to the dummy, and West plays the ten. You win with the king (or queen), come back to your hand, and lead another spade. This time West plays the ace. Now your other honor is good, and so are all of your little ones—*providing you have an entry.*

So you can see that the really big game is in the long suits. Just think what you can do with a six-card side suit in that dummy!

```
                    NORTH
                    ♠ A 6 5
                    ♡ 7 6 5
                    ◇ A 7 6 5 4 3
                    ♣ 2
      WEST                          EAST
      ♠ 9 8 7                       ♠ 4 3
      ♡ K Q J 9                     ♡ 10 4
      ◇ Q 9                         ◇ J 10 2
      ♣ K J 8 7                     ♣ A Q 10 9 4 3
                    SOUTH
                    ♠ K Q J 10 2
                    ♡ A 8 3 2
                    ◇ K 8
                    ♣ 6 5
```

South plays in 4 ♠ and West leads the king of hearts. This time South has three heart losers and two club losers. But wait! Look at that beautiful six-card diamond suit in the dummy. This is dummy's most valuable asset, and you must use it. Unfortunately, the diamonds are not all good. If they were, you could simply draw trumps and play your good diamonds. But these diamonds need to be established. What is the re-entry? The ace of spades. You must keep that ace of spades until the diamonds are good.

The plan is to win the first trick with the ace of hearts, then play the king of diamonds (high card from short side), then lead a diamond to the ace, and then trump a diamond. But be careful—trump the diamond with the ten of spades.

Now all three of the remaining diamonds in dummy are good. The next step is to draw trumps, ending in dummy. You play the king, the queen, and a low spade to dummy's ace. Be-

cause you received a normal 3-2 spade division, all of the opposing trumps are played, and so you can play your three good diamonds and discard three losers from your hand. In the end you
make an overtrick, but don't ask what would have happened if
you had drawn trumps first. You would have gone down two
tricks! A difference of three tricks from the actual result—the
difference being those three good diamonds.

We may now draw a few conclusions. *If the side suit in
dummy is already established, draw trumps and then use the
side suit. If the side suit in dummy needs establishment and the
only entries to dummy are in the trump suit, establish the side
suit and then draw trumps, ending in dummy.*

Bridge is a funny game. It is just as bad to draw trumps too
quickly as not to draw them at all.

Once you have grasped the idea that the long suit in dummy
is usually the first suit to be attacked, you will not be reluctant, as
declarer, to attack a suit which looks as sickly as this:

NORTH
♠ 8 7 6 5 4

WEST   EAST
♠ K J 10   ♠ A Q 9

SOUTH
♠ 3 2

Assume you have an eventual loser in an equally divided
suit (A x x facing K x x) and you must get rid of it somehow.
You look at your long suit in dummy and you see that pitiful
collection of spades. What should you do? *You should play them
immediately and set them up!* You must lead them twice to void
yourself; then you must go to the dummy and trump one. If they
divide 3-3, as they do in the diagram, the other two little ones will
be good. You must of course have an entry once they are established.

Here's a little problem for you. Taking the same suit, how
many entries would you need to establish the suit if the opposing
spades divided 4-2? The answer is three. You would have to get

over there twice to trump spades and once more to use the established spade.

Quiz time.

(a)   NORTH
    ♠ 8 6 3
    ♡ 7 5
    ◊ A 8 2
    ♣ A K J 3 2

        SOUTH
    ♠ A 4 2
    ♡ A 2
    ◊ K Q J 10 4
    ♣ Q 8 7

The contract is 6 ◊ and West leads the king of spades.

(a)   How many losers does South have?

(b)   Does he have any extra winners?

(c)   What should he do first: draw trumps or work on his long suit?

(b)   NORTH
    ♠ A Q 2
    ♡ A K 8 5 3
    ◊ 3 2
    ♣ 4 3 2

        SOUTH
    ♠ K J 10 9 4 3
    ♡ 4 2
    ◊ A 8
    ♣ A K 5

South plays in 6 ♠ and West leads the king of diamonds.

(a)   How many losers does South have?

(b)   Does he have any extra winners?

(c)   What should his plan be?
(d)   How would he play the same hand in a contract of
       4 ♠?

(c)   NORTH
           ♠ A 7 6 3 2
           ♡ K Q 10
           ◊ A 9 2
           ♣ 3 2

           SOUTH
           ♠ 4
           ♡ A J 9 8 7 6 5
           ◊ 8 7 6
           ♣ J 7

South plays in a contract of 4 ♡ and West takes the first
two club tricks and then leads the queen of diamonds.

(a)   How many losers does South have?
(b)   Does he have any extra winners?
(c)   Should he draw trumps?
(d)   What is his plan and what must he hope for?

(d)   NORTH
           ♠ K Q 2
           ♡ A 4 3
           ◊ A 7 6 5 4
           ♣ 7 6

           SOUTH
           ♠ J 3
           ♡ K Q J 10 8 7
           ◊ K 3 2
           ♣ Q 9

The contract is 4 ♡ and West takes the first two club tricks
and then leads the ten of diamonds.

(a)   How many losers does South have?
(b)   Does he have any extra winners?

(c)   Should he draw trumps?
(d)   Which suit should he play first?

(e)   NORTH
             ♠ A Q 6 4
             ♡ A 4 3
             ◊ A 7 6 5
             ♣ 7 6

             SOUTH
             ♠ 5 3
             ♡ K Q J 10 8 7
             ◊ K 3 2
             ♣ Q 9

South plays in a contract of 4 ♡ and the defense leads clubs. East winds up with the lead after the second club has been played. East returns a trump. South takes it with the king and plays the queen of trumps, each opponent following.

(a)   How many losers does South have?
(b)   Does he have any extra winners?
(c)   Which suit should he play first, spades or diamonds?

Solutions

(a)   South has three losers—two spades and one heart—but he also has two extra winners in clubs. He should win the ace of spades, draw trumps first because his extra winners are good and need not be established. After drawing trumps, he simply takes his five club tricks, along with his five diamond tricks and his two aces, to make the slam. This is a simple hand, but you should realize that some hands *are* simple. If the trumps are solid and the side suit good, relax—you are home free. Draw trumps and take your tricks.

(b)   South has two losers—one in clubs and one in dia-monds. He has a chance for one or even two extra winners in hearts. His plan should be to establish the hearts while the ace and queen of spades are still in dummy, waiting to be used as entries. The actual play would be to win the ace of diamonds, the ace and the king of hearts and then another heart, which he would trump in his hand. If the hearts divide 3-3, then the remaining hearts are high in dummy, and South should draw all of the outstanding trumps, ending in dummy. If, after trumping a heart (with a high spade, of course), he sees that the hearts were 4-2, then he enters dummy with the queen of spades and trumps another heart high. Then he plays two rounds of spades, ending in dummy, which allows him to use his established heart for a minor-suit discard.

In a contract of 4 ♠ South should draw trumps before monkeying around with the heart suit. He has a sure contract and need not take any risks.

(c)   In addition to the two clubs he has lost, South has two diamond losers. He also has a chance for an extra winner in spades. He has to do plenty of work with that spade suit in order to establish an extra winner. As a matter of fact, he must trump three spades in his own hand and hope that the opponents' spades were originally divided 4-3. If that is the case, he can make his game contract if he immediately starts in on the spades, using the hearts as future dummy entries. Under no circumstances should South draw trumps on this hand. The entries are more important than the potential nuisance of the few small hearts that the opponents have.

His play would be to win the first trick with the ace of diamonds, play the ace of spades, and then lead another spade, trumping it in his hand. He would then enter dummy in trumps and ruff another spade; back to dummy in trumps again and ruff a third spade. Assuming everything has gone according to plan, dummy's last spade is good, and South still has another heart entry in dummy so that he can use his

good spade. You should see how valuable it is to figure out in advance how many dummy entries you are
going to need. Otherwise, you will never know
whether you can afford to draw trumps or not.

(d)   South has four losers—two in clubs, one in spades,
and one in diamonds. He has a sure extra winner in
spades and two very likely extra winners in diamonds,
assuming a normal 3-2 division. The question is
whether South should establish the diamonds to throw
away the spades or establish the spade and throw
away the diamond. A moment's reflection ought to
give you the answer. If South establishes the diamonds, he must give up the lead to do so. Once the
opponents have the lead, they can play their ace of
spades for a total of four defensive tricks. But if South
knocks out the ace of spades, he can discard his losing diamond on dummy's good spade and end up
losing only three tricks. This is a fairly rare case—
establishing a shorter suit before a longer suit—but
the loser situation dictates the play.

(e)   In addition to the two clubs he has lost, South has
one loser in diamonds and a possible loser in spades.
He also has one potential extra winner in diamonds.
Remember, we said that any five-card suit might
turn out to be an extra winner. The same is true if
there is a total of seven cards between declarer and
dummy. Any seven cards. When declarer has a total
of seven cards, that leaves six cards in the opponents' hands. If those six cards are divided 3-3, the
hand that started with the four-card suit will have
an extra trick after the suit has been played three
times.

With this in mind, South should first play the
king, the ace, and a low card in diamonds to see if
the diamonds are divided 3-3 in the opponents'
hands. If they are, the fourth little diamond in
dummy will be good, and South will not have to risk
the spade finesse. If the diamonds do not divide 3-3,

he will have to try to avoid his spade loser via a finesse, leading low to the queen.

KEY POINTERS

(1) The key to roughly fifty percent or more of all suit contract play is long suit establishment.

(2) The key factors are losers, entries, and a decent trump suit.

(3) Declarer must always figure out in advance how many losers he must get rid of in order to make the hand and how many entries to dummy he needs to do this.

(4) If dummy has insufficient entries, declarer should look around for another way of getting rid of losers.

(5) One of the most likely suits in which dummy may have an entry or two to his long suit is the trump suit. This means that trumps must be drawn *after* the long suit has been established and declarer must *draw trumps ending in the dummy*.

(6) When establishing dummy's long suit before drawing trumps, be careful about trumping too low if you have a plentiful supply of high trumps.

(7) If dummy's suit is so strong that it does not need establishment, declarer normally draws trumps before using the suit.

(8) Creating extra winners will do you no good if the opponents have little trumps to use on your extra winners.

(9) Declarer must count both trumps and the suit that he is establishing in order to know exactly how many cards the opponents have in these suits at all times.

(10) When establishing dummy's long suit, you might keep in mind that if the opponents have started with an uneven number of cards in the suit (for example, six cards), they are most likely to divide unevenly (4-2). Conversely, if the opponents have started with an odd number of cards (for example, five cards), they are most likely to break as evenly as possible (3-2).

(11) Remember that the only reason why you are estab-

lishing dummy's long suit in the first place is because you have too many losers. If you can make your contract without establishing anything, go ahead and do so. The extra tricks are next to meaningless. Play your hands as safely as possible when you are in a secure contract and as optimistically as possible if you have too many losers.

11

Trumping in the Short Hand

♠ ♡ ◇ ♣

In the preceding chapter the technique of setting up dummy's long suit was analyzed. This is, of course, one of declarer's main ways of shedding losers in other suits.

Unfortunately, a great many hands that you will play will not have a long side suit in dummy, or there will be insufficient entries to dummy to attack the suit, or your trump suit will not be long enough or strong enough to establish dummy's length. Remember, you never want to be in a position where one of your opponents has more trumps than you do.

Fortunately, there is an alternate method of getting rid of losers. It appears on the scene when the declarer has a side suit which is longer in his hand than in the dummy. For example, assume you are playing the following hand in a contract of 4 ♡:

```
                NORTH
                ♠ 3 2
                ♡ 5 4
                ◇ A K 7 6 5
                ♣ 8 7 6 5

    WEST                        EAST
    ♠ Q 10 6 5                  ♠ J 9 8 7
    ♡ 3 2                       ♡ A 7 6
    ◇ J 9 8                     ◇ Q 10 2
    ♣ A K Q J                   ♣ 10 3 2

                SOUTH
                ♠ A K 4
                ♡ K Q J 10 9 8
                ◇ 4 3
                ♣ 9 4
```

West starts out with three rounds of clubs. You trump the third club and, as always, take stock of your losers. In this case you have a definite trump loser and a spade loser. Your diamonds are powerful, but it would be useless to try to establish them, as you have no re-entry to dummy once you do.

Take another look at your spade holding. Had the A K 4 been in the dummy and the 3 2 in your own hand, you would not have counted any losers in spades, because losers are counted from the long hand. In this case, however, you have more spades in your hand than in the dummy, and consequently, you have a loser.

Fortunately, the spades are unevenly divided between the two hands, which means you can work with the suit. If you play the ace, the king, and then the four of spades, you will be able to trump that loser in dummy and make your contract. It's that simple.

You have rid yourself of one of your losers by trumping in the short hand. You only had to be careful about drawing trumps prematurely. Had you played the king of hearts before trumping your spade, East might have taken the ace and returned a heart, removing dummy's last trump. Then you would have been stuck with your losing four of spades.

When trumping in the short hand, you must always ask yourself how many losers you are planning to trump and retain a sufficient number of trumps in the short hand (usually the dummy) for that purpose. For example, imagine that the spade holding on the above hand was:

NORTH
♠ 4

SOUTH
♠ A 5 3

You should figure two spade losers and keep at least two trumps in dummy in order to take care of those losers.

It should be pointed out before going any further that when you decide that the best way to rid yourself of your losers is to trump them in the dummy, you usually must defer drawing trumps, unless your dummy has enough trumps both to remove them from the opponents' hands and to take care of your own losers. For example, if you have one loser to trump in dummy and dummy has four trump cards, you can draw three rounds of trumps and then trump your loser. Usually, however, dummy has two or three trump cards, and you have two or three losers to trump, in which case drawing even one round of trump can be disastrous.

Also, you are no doubt thinking to yourself that it is rather risky to trump these losers, since one of your opponents might overtrump. True, but if you don't try to trump your losers, you will *always* be stuck with them. At least *most* of the time you can get rid of them by trumping them.

Assume for the moment that hearts are trump and that you have these holdings in spades:

(a) NORTH
    ♠ 7 6
    SOUTH
    ♠ 8 5 3

(b) NORTH
    ♠ 3
    SOUTH
    ♠ 8 7 6

(c) NORTH
    ♠ A 4
    SOUTH
    ♠ K 7 3

(d) NORTH
    ♠ A 5
    SOUTH
    ♠ 10 7 6 3

(e) NORTH
    ♠ A K 7 6
    SOUTH
    ♠ 8 4 2

How many losers do you count for yourself in spades in each of the examples? How many trump cards must you plan to retain in dummy to rid yourself of these losers?

Solutions

(a) You have three spade losers. Two are inevitable, but the third one can be trumped in dummy providing you play your spades before you remove all of dummy's trumps.

(b) Again, you have three spade losers, but this time you can rid yourself of two of them simply by leading a spade early to void the dummy and then trumping your remaining two spades.

(c)   This time you have one spade loser, and you must
      plan to keep one trump in dummy in order to dis-
      pose of it.

(d)   This time you have three losing spades, but two of
      them can be eliminated simply by playing the ace
      and conceding a spade. Once the dummy is void of
      spades, you can trump your remaining two spades.

(e)   This time you have one loser in spades, but when the
      dummy hand is as long or longer than your own
      hand in a particular suit, you cannot plan to trump
      in the dummy. This type of spade loser must be
      discarded on an extra winner from dummy if one
      happens to exist.

A few more words of caution may be necessary with re-
gard to trumping losers in the short hand. Study this diagram:

```
                    NORTH
                    ♠ 5 3
                    ♡ 10 4 3
                    ◊ 6 4 3
                    ♣ 8 7 5 3 2
    WEST                            EAST
    ♠ A Q 10                        ♠ K J 9 8 4
    ♡ 7 5 2                         ♡ 8 6
    ◊ J 9 8                         ◊ 10 7 5 2
    ♣ K Q J 9                       ♣ 10 6
                    SOUTH
                    ♠ 7 6 2
                    ♡ A K Q J 9
                    ◊ A K Q
                    ♣ A 4
```

South plays in 4 ♡ and West leads the king of clubs. How
many losers does South have? What should his plan be?

South should count three losers in spades and one in clubs,
for a total of four losers. His contract is 4 ♡ so he must elim-

inate one of his losers. Basically, there are two methods of eliminating losers, and both of them deal with *unevenly* divided side suits:

(1)   If dummy has a long side suit with entries, set up that suit by playing it until the opponents are exhausted (in that suit) and then discard the long hand's losers on the remaining cards after trumps have been removed.

(2)   When declarer has a longer side suit than dummy, play that suit until dummy is void and then trump in the dummy the declarer's remaining losers in that suit.

On this hand it should be clear that you cannot establish the club suit, as there is a shortage of dummy entries. Therefore, you must follow the second method, which is trumping your spade loser in dummy.

How many trumps do you need in dummy to dispose of your spade loser or losers? You need only one because after you concede two spade tricks to the opponents, dummy will be void and you will have only one spade remaining.

Now we come to the point of this hand. If you think to yourself that you need only one trump in dummy in order to dispose of your spade loser, you might delude yourself into thinking that you can draw two rounds of trumps, leaving one trump in dummy. Do you see what will happen if you do this? When you finally get around to playing spades, your opponents, unless they are the friendly type, will simply lead their last trump, removing your last trump from dummy and preventing you from trumping your spade loser.

Whenever you are planning to void dummy in a side suit with the intention of trumping your losers in the dummy, you must assume that each time the opponents have the lead they will lead a trump. It is in their best interest to do so.

On the above hand you are going to have to lead spades twice in order to void dummy of spades. This means that the opponents will have two opportunities to lead a trump. That is still okay, as you will have a third trump to take care of your losing spade. But notice what would happen if you had drawn just one little trump first: the opponents would have been able to lead trump two more times and you would have ended up without a trump in dummy to take care of your spade loser.

You may have noticed that in this chapter we have been dealing exclusively with trumping cards in the dummy or the short hand. Basically, is there any difference between trumping in the long hand and in the short hand? Assume for the moment that hearts are trump and that this is your trump suit:

NORTH (short hand)
♡ 7 6 5

WEST   EAST
♡ 10 9 8   ♡ 4 3

SOUTH (long hand)
♡ A K Q J 2

If you were simply to remove the opponents' trumps (and your dummy's) by playing the ace, king, and queen, you would end up with the jack and the deuce and take a total of five trump tricks.

Now let's see what would happen if before playing the ace, king, and queen of hearts, you were to trump something with your deuce of trump. Would you gain an extra trick? No. Your deuce was good anyway after you drew the opponent's trump, wasn't it? So you have gained nothing by trumping with your deuce.

Yet this is one of the most common of all errors made by beginning players. They invariably think that if they trump something with a small card, they are gaining a trick. They forget that if they had drawn trumps first, their little trumps would have been good anyway.

Trumping in the long hand does not give declarer any extra tricks. The main reason for trumping in the long hand is to establish dummy's long suit. On the other hand, declarer may have to trump in the long hand because the opponents have forced him to do so. Or he may want to re-enter his hand immediately, and the only way to do so would be to trump a card in the long hand. It is a common play, but it must be understood that declarer is not gaining any trump tricks by doing so.

This may shock you, but very often the defender's best play is to force declarer to trump in the long hand. In this way the defenders have a good chance of winding up with more trumps than the declarer.

However, this chapter is dealing with trumping in the short hand. Back to our original trump suit:

NORTH (short hand)
♡ 7 6 5

WEST   EAST
♡ 10 9 8   ♡ 4 3

SOUTH (long hand)
♡ A K Q J 2

Assume for the moment that declarer has a small spade in his hand and that dummy is void in spades. Assume that declarer leads that spade and trumps it with dummy's five of hearts. Is there any difference between that and trumping a spade from dummy with declarer's deuce of hearts? Don't leave this chapter until you see the difference.

When you trump a spade with dummy's five of hearts, you still retain the A K Q J 2 of hearts in your own hand, which is worth five tricks. Besides these five tricks you make a trick with dummy's five of hearts—for a total of six tricks! What if you had two spades in your hand and dummy was void? You could then trump them both and still have your five heart tricks in your own hand. In other words, *each time declarer trumps a loser in the short hand he gains a full trick.*

Now you should see why declarer should always consider the possibility of trumping losers in the short hand. Of course, in order to do this, declarer must have a short suit in dummy and must hold more cards in that suit in his own hand. It should go without saying that if declarer and dummy both have the same number of cards in a side suit or if dummy is longer, this play cannot be contemplated.

Finally, there is the technique for reducing an evenly divided suit to an unevenly divided suit!

See if you can see any difference between these two hands (in each case the contract is 4 ♡ and the lead is the queen of spades):

(1)   NORTH
       ♠ A 3 2
       ♡ 9 3 2
       ◊ 5 4 3 2
       ♣ A K Q

(2)   NORTH
       ♠ A 3 2
       ♡ 9 3 2
       ◊ 6 5 4 3 2
       ♣ 3 2

SOUTH
♠ K 5 4
♡ A K Q J 10
◊ 8 7 6
♣ 3 2

SOUTH
♠ K 5 4
♡ K Q J 10 8
◊ 8 7
♣ A K Q

Beginning with the first hand, we have one spade loser and three diamond losers. However, to compensate for our four losers, we have an extra winner in clubs. Notice that the extra winner is in dummy, and so declarer can throw away a loser from the *long hand* on the extra club winner.

Playing the first hand, declarer can simply win the spade lead in his own hand, draw trumps, and discard a loser on the queen of clubs. This will reduce declarer's losers to three, or, to look at it the other way, declarer will simply take the first ten tricks—five hearts, two spades, and three clubs.

Now study the second hand. Once again, declarer has four losers—one spade, one trump, and two diamonds. And again there is an extra winner in clubs. The only difference is that the extra winner is in the long hand.

When the extra winner is in the long hand, a two-step process is necessary when playing that suit.

(1) On the extra winner discard a loser from dummy (making an evenly divided suit unevenly divided).

(2) Trump any loser in the short hand.

Therefore, on the second hand we win the spade, preferably in dummy, and play three rounds of clubs, discarding a spade from dummy. Then we play the king of spades and trump a spade in the dummy.

Notice how much more involved the process becomes when the extra winners are in the long hand. Notice also in this hand how we changed an even distribution into an uneven distribution by discarding a spade from dummy on a club.

When declarer uses an extra winner from dummy to discard a loser from his hand, that is a one-step process. When the extra winner comes from declarer's hand, he must still trump a loser in the short hand.

Time to show off.

(a) NORTH
♠ A 4 3 2
♡ 9 2
◊ A 7 6 5 4
♣ 3 2

SOUTH
♠ 8 7 6
♡ A K Q J 10
◊ 8 3
♣ A K 4

Contract: 4 ♡
Opening lead: King of diamonds

(b) NORTH
♠ 7
♡ 3 2
◊ A 8 7 6 4
♣ 7 6 5 4 3

SOUTH
♠ 9 6
♡ A K Q J 10 9 8
◊ K 5
♣ A K

Contract: 6 ♡
Opening lead: Queen of diamonds

(c)   NORTH
            ♠ A 4
            ♡ K 7 6
            ◊ 10 8 7 6 5
            ♣ 7 6 5

            SOUTH
            ♠ K Q 3
            ♡ Q J 10 9 8 2
            ◊ 2
            ♣ A 9 3

Contract: 4 ♡
Opening lead: King of clubs

On each of the three above hands, count your losers and formulate a plan. Decide whether you can afford to draw trumps or not, and if not, which suit you should be attacking.

Solutions

(a) You have four losers—two in spades, one in diamonds, and one in clubs. The easiest way to rid yourself of one loser is to win the first trick with the ace of diamonds and play the ace, king, and four of clubs, trumping the four with the nine of hearts, which cannot be overtrumped. Then you should draw trumps, and you will easily make your contract. Notice that by trumping a club in dummy, you make six trump tricks (five in your own hand plus the club ruff in dummy).

(b) You have two losers, both in spades. Your first play after taking the first trick with the king or ace of diamonds should be a spade. You must void your dummy in spades so that you can trump your losing spade in dummy. It would be a fatal error to draw even one round of trump on this hand, because the opponents, upon gaining the lead in spades, could play a second round of trumps and leave you stranded with two spade losers instead of one.

(c)   You have four losers—a trump, a diamond, and two clubs. Fortunately, you have an extra winner in spades, but it is in the long hand, which means you must do some work. You should win the first trick with the ace of clubs and then play three rounds of spades, discarding a club from dummy. Having done that, you will be left with one club in dummy and two in your hand. You must then lead a club, voiding dummy in clubs so that you can eventually trump your club loser in dummy. This is another hand in which you cannot afford to draw trumps until you trump your club loser.

KEY POINTERS

(1)   The long hand is the hand which begins with the most trump cards. Trumping in the long hand does not gain the declarer any extra tricks.

(2)   The short hand, normally the dummy hand, is the hand which begins with fewer trump cards. Each time declarer trumps a loser in the short hand, he gains an extra trick.

(3)   In order to trump a loser in the short hand, the declarer must have a side suit which is longer than that corresponding suit in dummy. In this case declarer simply voids dummy in that suit and trumps his losers in dummy.

(4)   Declarer must be on the lookout for extra winners in both hands. If the extra winners are in dummy, declarer simply discards his own losers on them. However, if the extra winners are in the declarer's hand, he must go through a two-step process: (1) play his extra winners with the intention of making an equally divided side suit unequally divided (by shortening dummy) and (2) trump in dummy his own losers in that suit. See the second quiz hand.

(5)   Declarer must always keep in mind that when he is trumping in the short hand, the opponents can see what he is trying to do and will usually play trumps at every opportunity in order to foil him. It is for that reason that declarer can seldom afford to draw trumps when his plan is to trump losers in the dummy.

(6)   Just as in notrump contracts, declarer simply cannot be afraid to give up the lead before he draws trumps. If losers must be trumped in the dummy, then that suit must be played early, and this often means giving up the lead once or twice before drawing trumps. Don't worry—you are playing the hand properly.

(7)   When trumping two or three losers in the dummy, you usually use your smaller trumps at the beginning. You can use higher trumps later, when the opponents are also running out of the suit.

Index

Ace in notrump play, 40, 44

Bath Coup, 48

Counting by fours, 118
Counting losers in trump play, 77-89, 128
   immediate vs. eventual losers, 82, 87
Counting tricks in notrump play
   sure tricks, 3-8
   tricks to be established, 10-11
Counting trumps, 74-76

Danger hand in notrump play, 59-69
   definition of, 61
   finesses and, 64-65, 68
Drawing trumps, 74-76
   before or after playing extra winners, 81-82, 88
   long suit establishment and, 114-15, 128
   when declarer plans to trump losers in dummy, 141
"Ducking" in notrump play, 21
   See also Hold-up play
Dummy
   entry into, in establishing long suits, 114-20, 128-29
   even and uneven division of suits between declarer and, 93-94
     in finessing, 98-99, 111
   trumping losers in, 141

Equal cards, playing of, 15
Establishing extra winners
   by establishing long suits, 113-29
   by force, 91-96
Establishing tricks in notrump play, 9-15
   by finessing, 37
   by hold-up play, 48
   in long suits, 17-24
   to precede taking of sure tricks, 12-15
Evenly vs. unevenly divided suits
   in trump play, 93-94
   finessing and, 98-99, 111
Extra winners in trump play, 91-111
   created by establishing long suits, 113-29
   created by finessing, 96-105
   definition of, 87
   established by force, 91-96
   three types of, 111
   throwing losers on, 79, 88, 128
   when in long hand, 138
   whether played before or after drawing trump, 81-82, 88

Finessing
   in notrump play, 25-37
     into non-danger hand, 64-65, 68
     repeated finessing, 26-27
     rules for, 26, 32
   in trump play, 96-111

Finessing (*Cont.*)
    with no losers in the suit, 102-5
    repeated finessing, 100-1, 111
    unevenly divided vs. evenly divided suits, 98-99, 111
Free finesses, 103-5, 111

Hold-up play, 39-49
  Bath Coup, 48
Honors, rule in leading of, 32

Lead, the
  giving up of
    in notrump play, 15, 21
    in trump play, 144
  rule of eleven applied to, 49-58
  of top of nothing, 54, 58
  when to lead honors, 32
Long hand
  counting losers from, 78, 87
  definition of, 78
  trumping of, 136, 141
Long suits
  in notrump play, 17-24, 37
    countered by hold-up policy, 39-49
  in trump play, 113-29
Losers in trump play
  counting of, 77-89, 128
    immediate vs. eventual losers, 82, 87
  getting rid of
    by throwing on extra winners, 79, 88, 128
    by trumping in short hand, 131-42
Low cards, taking tricks with
  in notrump play, 17-24
  in trump play, by establishing long suits, 113-29

Non-danger hand, *see* Danger hand
Notrump play
  danger hand in, 59-69
    definition, 61
    finesses and, 64-65, 68
  defenders' leads in

    leads from short suits, 60
    rule of eleven and, 49-58
    of top of nothing, 54, 58
  difference between trump play and, 73-76
  establishing tricks in, 9-15
    by finessing, 37
    by hold-up play, 48
    in long suits, 17-24
    to precede taking of sure tricks, 12-15
  finessing in, 25-37
    into non-danger hand, 64-65, 68
    repeated finessing, 26-27
    rules for, 26, 32
  first suit to play in, 14-15
  giving up the lead in, 15, 21
  hold-up play in, 39-49
    Bath Coup, 48
  playing equal cards in, 15
  rule of eleven in, 25-37
  sure tricks in
    counting of, 3-8
    to be taken after you have established, 12-15
  taking tricks with spot-cards in, 17-24

Repeatable finesses
  in notrump play, 26-27
  in trump play, 100-2, 111
Ruff, defined, 76
Rule of eleven, 49-58

Short hand
  definition of, 78
  trumping in, 131-42
Spot-cards, taking tricks with
  in notrump play, 17-24
  in trump play, by establishing long suits, 113-29
Suit contracts, *see* Trump play
Sure tricks in notrump play
  counting of, 3-8
  to be taken after you have established, 12-15

INDEX

Top of nothing, lead of, 54, 58
Trump play (suit contracts)
  counting losers in, 77-89, 128
    immediate vs. eventual losers,
      82, 87
  counting trumps in, 74-76
  defenders' leads of trump in, 135,
    141
  difference between notrump play
    and, 73-76
  drawing trumps in, 74-76
    before or after playing extra
      winners, 81-82, 88
    long suit establishment and,
      114-15, 128
    when declarer plans to trump
      losers in dummy, 141
  extra winners in, 91-111
    created by establishing long
      suits, 113-29
    created by finessing, 96-105
    definition of, 87

    established by force, 91-96
    three types, 111
    throwing losers on, 79, 88, 128
    when in long hand, 138
    whether played before or after
      drawing trump, 81-82, 88
  giving up the lead in, 144
  risk of going down extra tricks
    vs. making contract, 104,
    111
  rule of eleven in, 58
  same hand played at different
    levels, 89
  trumping in short hand, 131-42
Trumping
  defined, 76
  rule for, 75
  in short hand, 131-42

Voids in trump play, free finesses
  and, 104-5

An Unforgettable Treasure
Of Laughter and Wisdom

The Knight in Rusty Armor

2 MILLION COPIES SOLD WORLDWIDE

This story is guaranteed to captivate your imagination as it helps you discover the secret of what is most important in life. It's a delightful tale of a desperate knight in search of his true self.

The Knight in Rusty Armor by Robert Fisher is one of Wilshire Book Company's most popular titles. It's available in numerous languages and has become an international bestseller.

Join the knight as he faces a life-changing dilemma upon discovering that he is trapped in his armor, just as we may be trapped in *our* armor—an invisible one we put on to protect ourselves from others and from various aspects of life.

As the knight searches for a way to free himself, he receives guidance from the wise sage Merlin the Magician, who encourages him to embark on the most difficult crusade of his life. The knight takes up the challenge and travels the Path of Truth, where he meets his real self for the first time and confronts the Universal Truths that govern his life—and ours.

The knight's journey reflects our own, filled with hope and despair, belief and disillusionment, laughter and tears. His insights become our insights as we follow along on his intriguing adventure of self-discovery. Anyone who has ever struggled with the meaning of life and love will discover profound wisdom and truth as this unique fantasy unfolds.

The Knight in Rusty Armor will expand your mind, touch your heart, and nourish your soul.

The Knight in Rusty Armor Music Tape

Treat yourself to the soundtrack of the musical production of *The Knight in Rusty Armor*, narrated by Robert Fisher.

I invite you to meet an extraordinary princess and accompany her on an enlightening journey. You will laugh with her and cry with her, learn with her and grow with her . . . and she will become a dear friend you will never forget.

Marcia Grad Powers

1 MILLION COPIES SOLD WORLDWIDE

The Princess Who Believed in Fairy Tales

"Here is a very special book that will guide you lovingly into a new way of thinking about yourself and your life so that the future will be filled with hope and love and song."

OG MANDINO
Author, *The Greatest Salesman in the World*

The Princess Who Believed in Fairy Tales by Marcia Grad is a personal growth book of the rarest kind. It's a delightful, humor-filled story you will experience so deeply that it can literally change your feelings about yourself, your relationships, and your life.

The princess's journey of self-discovery on the Path of Truth is an eye-opening, inspiring, empowering psychological and spiritual journey that symbolizes the one we all take through life as we separate illusion from reality, come to terms with our childhood dreams and pain, and discover who we really are and how life works.

If you have struggled with childhood pain, with feelings of not being good enough, with the loss of your dreams, or if you have been disappointed in your relationships, this book will prove to you that happy endings—and new beginnings—are always possible. Or, if you simply wish to get closer to your own truth, the princess will guide you.

The universal appeal of this book has resulted in its translation into numerous languages.

Excerpts from Readers' Heartfelt Letters

"*The Princess* is truly a gem! Though I've read a zillion self-help and spiritual books, I got more out of this one than from any other one I've ever read. It is just too illuminating and full of wisdom to ever be able to thank you enough. The friends and family I've given copies to have raved about it."

"*The Princess* is powerful, insightful, and beautifully written. I am seventy years old and have seldom encountered greater wisdom. I've been waiting to read this book my entire life. You are a psychologist, a guru, a saint, and an angel all wrapped up into one. I thank you with all my heart."

Available wherever books are sold or send $12.00 (CA res. $12.99) plus $2.00 S/H to Wilshire Book Co., 9731 Variel Avenue, Chatsworth, California 91311-4315

For our complete catalog, visit our Web site at www.mpowers.com.

The Magic of Getting What You Want

Here is the book that could well become your blueprint for personal fulfillment. It was written by one of the foremost authorities on motivation, the author of that enormously successful book *The Magic of Thinking Success*, which has sold more than one million copies.

Now, in this immensely readable, practical, and comforting volume, Dr. Schwartz tells us how we can have more wealth, influence, and happiness by approaching life positively and planning our goals creatively. Dr. Schwartz emphasizes that, after analyzing our special assets and capabilities and deciding what we should do with them, we must also be willing to make certain personal adjustments to get what we want.

Although most of us know what we should be doing with our lives, we need to be reminded of the many ways in which others have achieved their goals. This down-to-earth book is a veritable treasury of inspiration and practical suggestions for everyone who wants to develop a winning philosophy—and, as Dr. Schwartz believes, "a winning philosophy always produces winners."

Find out how to

- Turn your dreams into attainable goals
- Make your mental vision work for you
- Feel confident in any business or social situation
- Win others to your way of thinking

The way you lived yesterday determined your today. But the way you live today will determine your tomorrow. Every day is a new opportunity to become the way you want to be and to have your life become what you want it to be.

Take the first step toward becoming all you're capable of being. Read *The Magic of Getting What You Want* and follow the proven step-by-step plan that can help anyone develop the ultimate in personal power. Then get ready for an incredible adventure that will change you and your life forever.

Available wherever books are sold or send $15.00 (CA res. $16.24) plus $2.00 S/H to Wilshire Book Co., 9731 Variel Ave., Chatsworth, CA 91311.

For our complete catalog, visit our Web site at www.mpowers.com.

Treat Yourself to This Fun, Inspirational Book and Discover How to
Find Happiness and Serenity . . . No Matter What Life Dishes Out

The Dragon Slayer
With a Heavy Heart

*This new book by bestselling author Marcia Powers promises to be
one of the most important you will ever read—and one of the most
entertaining, uplifting, and memorable.*

*It brings the Serenity Prayer—which for years has been the guiding
light of 12-step programs worldwide—to everyone . . . and teaches
both new and longtime devotees how to apply it most effectively to
their lives.*

Sometimes things happen we wish hadn't. Sometimes things *don't*
happen we wish *would*. In the course of living, problems arise, both
big and small. We might wish our past had been different or that *we*
could be different. We struggle through disappointments and
frustrations, losses and other painful experiences.

As hard as we may try to be strong, to have a good attitude, not to
let things get us down, we don't always succeed. We get upset. We
worry. We feel stressed. We get depressed. We get angry. We do the
best we can and wait for things to *get* better so we can *feel* better. In
the meantime, our hearts may grow heavy . . . perhaps very heavy.

That's what happened to Duke the Dragon Slayer. In fact, *his*
heart grew *so* heavy with all that was wrong, with all that was not the
way it should be, with all that was unfair, that he became desperate to
lighten it—and set forth on the Path of Serenity to find out how.

Accompany Duke on this life-changing adventure. His guides will
be your guides. His answers will be your answers. His tools will be
your tools. His success will be your success. And by the time he is
heading home, both Duke and you will know how to take life's inevitable lumps and bumps in stride—and find happiness and serenity
anytime . . . even when you really, REALLY wish some things were
different.

"A BEAUTIFUL, EXCEPTIONALLY WELL-WRITTEN STORY THAT CAN HELP
EVERYONE TO BECOME EMOTIONALLY STRONGER AND BETTER ABLE TO
COPE WITH ADVERSITY."   Albert Ellis, Ph.D.
President, Albert Ellis Institute
Author of *A Guide to Rational Living*

Books by Melvin Powers

HOW TO GET RICH IN MAIL ORDER

1. How to Develop Your Mail Order Expertise 2. How to Find a Unique Product or Service to Sell 3. How to Make Money with Classified Ads 4. How to Make Money with Display Ads 5. The Unlimited Potential for Making Money with Direct Mail 6. How to Copycat Successful Mail Order Operations 7. How I Created a Bestseller Using the Copycat Technique 8. How to Start and Run a Profitable Mail Order Special Interest Book Business 9. I Enjoy Selling Books by Mail—Some of My Successful Ads 10. Five of My Most Successful Direct Mail Pieces That Sold and Are Selling Millions of Dollars' Worth of Books 11. Melvin Powers's Mail Order Success Strategy—Follow it and You'll Become a Millionaire 12. How to Sell Your Products to Mail Order Companies, Retail Outlets, Jobbers, and Fund Raisers for Maximum Distribution and Profit 13. How to Get Free Display Ads and Publicity that Will Put You on the Road to Riches 14. How to Make Your Advertising Copy Sizzle 15. Questions and Answers to Help You Get Started Making Money 16. A Personal Word from Melvin Powers 17. How to Get Started 18. Selling Products on Television

8½" x 11½" — 352 Pages . . . $20.00

MAKING MONEY WITH CLASSIFIED ADS

1. Getting Started with Classified Ads 2. Everyone Loves to Read Classified Ads 3. How to Find a Money-Making Product 4. How to Write Classified Ads that Make Money 5. What I've Learned from Running Thousands of Classified Ads 6. Classified Ads Can Help You Make Big Money in Multi-Level Programs 7. Two-Step Classified Ads Made Me a Multi-Millionaire—They Can Do the Same for You! 8. One-Inch Display Ads Can Work Wonders 9. Display Ads Can Make You a Fortune Overnight 10. Although I Live in California, I Buy My Grapefruit from Florida 11. Nuts and Bolts of Mail Order Success 12. What if You Can't Get Your Business Running Successfully? What's Wrong? How to Correct it 13. Strategy for Mail Order Success

8½" x 11½" — 240 Pages . . . $20.00

HOW TO SELF-PUBLISH YOUR BOOK AND HAVE THE FUN AND EXCITEMENT OF BEING A BEST-SELLING AUTHOR

1. Who is Melvin Powers? 2. What is the Motivation Behind Your Decision to Publish Your Book? 3. Why You Should Read This Chapter Even if You Already Have an Idea for a Book 4. How to Test the Salability of Your Book Before You Write One Word 5. How I Achieved Sales Totaling $2,000,000 on My Book *How to Get Rich in Mail Order* 6. How to Develop a Second Career by Using Your Expertise 7. How to Choose an Enticing Book Title 8. Marketing Strategy 9. Success Stories 10. How to Copyright Your Book 11. How to Write a Winning Advertisement 12. Advertising that Money Can't Buy 13. Questions and Answers to Help You Get Started 14. Self-Publishing and the Midas Touch   8½" x 11½" — 240 Pages . . . $20.00

A PRACTICAL GUIDE TO SELF-HYPNOSIS

1. What You Should Know about Self-Hypnosis 2. What about the Dangers of Hypnosis? 3. Is Hypnosis the Answer? 4. How Does Self-Hypnosis Work? 5. How to Arouse Yourself From the Self-Hypnotic State 6. How to Attain Self-Hypnosis 7. Deepening the Self-Hypnotic State 8. What You Should Know about Becoming an Excellent Subject 9. Techniques for Reaching the Somnambulistic State 10. A New Approach to Self-Hypnosis 11. Psychological Aids and Their Function 12. Practical Applications of Self-Hypnosis   144 Pages . . . $10.00

Available wherever books are sold or from the publisher.
Please add $2.00 shipping and handling for each book ordered.

WILSHIRE BOOK COMPANY

9731 Variel Avenue, Chatsworth, California 91311
For our complete catalog, visit our Web site at www.mpowers.com.

Books by Albert Ellis, Ph.D.

A GUIDE TO RATIONAL LIVING
1.5 Million Copies Sold

1. How Far Can You Go with Self-Therapy? 2. You Largely Feel the Way You Think 3. Feeling Well by Thinking Straight 4. How You Create Your Feelings 5. Thinking Yourself Out of Emotional Disturbances 6. Recognizing and Reducing Neurotic Behavior 7. Overcoming the Influences of the Past 8. Is Reason Always Reasonable? 9. Refusing to Feel Desperately Unhappy 10. Tackling Your Dire Need for Approval 11. Reducing Your Dire Fears of Failure 12. How to Start Blaming and Start Living 13. How to Feel Frustrated but Not Depressed or Enraged 14. Controlling Your Own Emotional Destiny 15. Conquering Anxiety and Panic 16. Acquiring Self-Discipline 17. Rewriting Your Personal History 18. Accepting and Coping with the Grim Facts of Life 19. Overcoming Inertia and Getting Creatively Absorbed   304 Pages . . . $15.00

A GUIDE TO PERSONAL HAPPINESS

1. Why Search for Personal Happiness? 2. ABC's of Personal Happiness 3. Main Blocks to Personal Happiness 4. Disputing and Uprooting Emotional Disturbance 5. Emotive Methods of Achieving Personal Happiness 6. Behavioral Methods of Achieving Personal Happiness 7. Ten Rules for Achieving Personal Happiness 8. Overcoming Shyness and Feelings of Inadequacy 9. Overcoming Feelings of Guilt 10. Coping with Depression and Low Frustration Tolerance 11. Coping with Anger and with Mating Problems 12. Overcoming Sex Problems 13. Coping with Work Problems 14. Summing Up: Eliminating Your Self-Created Roadblocks to Personal Happiness 15. Upward and Onward to Self-Actualizing and Joy

144 Pages . . . $10.00

HOW TO LIVE WITH A NEUROTIC

1. The Possibility of Helping Troubled People 2. How to Recognize a Person with Emotional Disturbance 3. How Emotional Disturbances Originate 4. Some Basic Factors in Emotional Upsets 5. How to Help a Neurotic Overcome Disturbance 6. How to Live with a Person Who Remains Neurotic 7. How to Live with Yourself Though You Fail to Help a Neurotic   160 Pages . . . $10.00

HOW TO RAISE AN EMOTIONALLY HEALTHY, HAPPY CHILD

1. Neurotics Are Born as Well as Made 2. What Is a Neurotic Child? 3. Helping Children Overcome Fears and Anxieties 4. Helping Children with Problems of Achievement 5. Helping Children Overcome Hostility 6. Helping Children Become Self-Disciplined 7. Helping Children with Sex Problems 8. Helping Children with Conduct Problems 9. Helping Children with Personal Behavior Problems 10. How to Live with a Neurotic Child and Like It   256 Pages . . . $10.00

A GUIDE TO SUCCESSFUL MARRIAGE

1. Modern Marriage: Hotbed of Neurosis 2. Factors Causing Marital Disturbance 3. Gauging Marital Compatibility 4. Problem Solving in Marriage 5. Can We Be Intelligent About Marriage? 6. Love or Infatuation? 7. To Marry or Not to Marry 8. Sexual Preparation for Marriage 9. Impotence in the Male 10. Frigidity in the Female 11. Sex Excess 12. Controlling Sex Impulses 13. Non-monogamous Desires 14. Communication in Marriage 15. Children 16. In-Laws 17. Marital Incompatibility Versus Neurosis 18. Divorce 19. Succeeding in Marriage

304 Pages . . . $10.00

WILSHIRE SELF-IMPROVEMENT LIBRARY

ASTROLOGY

___ASTROLOGY—HOW TO CHART YOUR HOROSCOPE Max Heindel 7.00
___ASTROLOGY AND SEXUAL ANALYSIS Morris C. Goodman 10.00
___ASTROLOGY AND YOU Carroll Righter 5.00
___ASTROLOGY MADE EASY Astarte 7.00
___ASTROLOGY, ROMANCE, YOU AND THE STARS Anthony Norvell 10.00
___MY WORLD OF ASTROLOGY Sydney Omarr 10.00
___THOUGHT DIAL Sydney Omarr. 7.00
___WHAT THE STARS REVEAL ABOUT THE MEN IN YOUR LIFE Thelma White 3.00

BRIDGE

___BRIDGE BIDDING MADE EASY Edwin B. Kantar 15.00
___BRIDGE CONVENTIONS Edwin B. Kantar 10.00
___COMPETITIVE BIDDING IN MODERN BRIDGE Edgar Kaplan 7.00
___DEFENSIVE BRIDGE PLAY COMPLETE Edwin B Kantar 20.00
___GAMESMAN BRIDGE—PLAY BETTER WITH KANTAR Edwin B. Kantar 7.00
___HOW TO IMPROVE YOUR BRIDGE Alfred Sheinwold 7.00
___IMPROVING YOUR BIDDING SKILLS Edwin B. Kantar 10.00
___INTRODUCTION TO DECLARER'S PLAY Edwin B. Kantar 15.00
___INTRODUCTION TO DEFENDER'S PLAY Edwin B. Kantar 15.00
___KANTAR FOR THE DEFENSE Edwin B. Kantar 10.00
___KANTAR FOR THE DEFENSE VOLUME 2 Edwin B. Kantar 10.00
___TEST YOUR BRIDGE PLAY Edwin B. Kantar 10.00
___VOLUME 2—TEST YOUR BRIDGE PLAY Edwin B. Kantar 10.00
___WINNING DECLARER PLAY Dorothy Hayden Truscott 10.00

BUSINESS, STUDY & REFERENCE

___BRAINSTORMING Charles Clark 10.00
___CONVERSATION MADE EASY Elliot Russell 5.00
___EXAM SECRET Dennis B. Jackson 7.00
___FIX-IT BOOK Arthur Symons 2.00
___HOW TO DEVELOP A BETTER SPEAKING VOICE M. Hellier 5.00
___HOW TO SAVE 50% ON GAS & CAR EXPENSES Ken Stansbie 1.00
___HOW TO SELF-PUBLISH YOUR BOOK & MAKE IT A BEST SELLER Melvin Powers . 20.00
___INCREASE YOUR LEARNING POWER Geoffrey A. Dudley 5.00
___PRACTICAL GUIDE TO BETTER CONCENTRATION Melvin Powers 5.00
___7 DAYS TO FASTER READING William S. Schaill 7.00
___SONGWRITER'S RHYMING DICTIONARY Jane Shaw Whitfield 15.00
___SPELLING MADE EASY Lester D. Basch & Dr. Milton Finkelstein 3.00
___STUDENT'S GUIDE TO BETTER GRADES J.A. Rickard 3.00
___YOUR WILL & WHAT TO DO ABOUT IT Attorney Samuel G. King 1.00

CHESS & CHECKERS

___BEGINNER'S GUIDE TO WINNING CHESS Fred Reinfeld 10.00
___CHESS IN TEN EASY LESSONS Larry Evans 10.00
___CHESS MADE EASY Milton L. Hanauer 5.00
___CHESS PROBLEMS FOR BEGINNERS Edited by Fred Reinfeld 7.00
___CHESS TACTICS FOR BEGINNERS Edited by Fred Reinfeld 10.00
___HOW TO WIN AT CHECKERS Fred Reinfeld 10.00
___1001 BRILLIANT WAYS TO CHECKMATE Fred Reinfeld 12.00
___1001 WINNING CHESS SACRIFICES & COMBINATIONS Fred Reinfeld 15.00

COOKERY & HERBS

___CULPEPER'S HERBAL REMEDIES Dr. Nicholas Culpeper 5.00
___HEALING POWER OF HERBS May Bethel 5.00
___HEALING POWER OF NATURAL FOODS May Bethel 7.00
___HOME GARDEN COOKBOOK—DELICIOUS NATURAL FOOD RECIPES Ken Kraft . . 3.00

_____MEATLESS MEAL GUIDE Tomi Ryan & James H. Ryan, M.D. 4.00
_____VEGETABLE GARDENING FOR BEGINNERS Hugh Wilberg 2.00
_____VEGETABLES FOR TODAY'S GARDENS R. Milton Carleton 2.00
_____VEGETARIAN COOKERY Janet Walker 10.00
_____VEGETARIAN COOKING MADE EASY & DELECTABLE Veronica Vezza 3.00

GAMBLING & POKER

_____HOW TO WIN AT POKER Terence Reese & Anthony T. Watkins 10.00
_____SCARNE ON DICE John Scarne 20.00
_____WINNING AT CRAPS Dr. Lloyd T. Commins 10.00
_____WINNING AT GIN Chester Wander & Cy Rice 10.00
_____WINNING AT POKER—AN EXPERT'S GUIDE John Archer 10.00
_____WINNING AT 21—AN EXPERT'S GUIDE John Archer 10.00
_____WINNING POKER SYSTEMS Norman Zadeh 10.00

HEALTH

_____COPING WITH ALZHEIMER'S Rose Oliver, Ph.D. & Francis Bock, Ph.D. 10.00
_____HELP YOURSELF TO BETTER SIGHT Margaret Darst Corbett 10.00
_____HOW YOU CAN STOP SMOKING PERMANENTLY Ernest Caldwell 1.00
_____NEW CARBOHYDRATE DIET COUNTER Patti Lopez-Pereira 2.00
_____REFLEXOLOGY Dr. Maybelle Segal 7.00
_____REFLEXOLOGY FOR GOOD HEALTH Anna Kaye & Don C. Matchan 10.00
_____YOU CAN LEARN TO RELAX Dr. Samuel Gutwirth 5.00

HOBBIES

_____BEACHCOMBING FOR BEGINNERS Norman Hickin 2.00
_____BLACKSTONE'S MODERN CARD TRICKS Harry Blackstone 7.00
_____BLACKSTONE'S SECRETS OF MAGIC Harry Blackstone 7.00
_____ENTERTAINING WITH ESP Tony 'Doc' Shiels 2.00
_____400 FASCINATING MAGIC TRICKS YOU CAN DO Howard Thurston 10.00
_____HOW I TURN JUNK INTO FUN AND PROFIT Sari 3.00
_____HOW TO BRING UP YOUR PET DOG Kurt Unkelbach 2.00
_____HOW TO WRITE A HIT SONG AND SELL IT Tommy Boyce 10.00
_____MAGIC FOR ALL AGES Walter Gibson 10.00
_____STAMP COLLECTING FOR BEGINNERS Burton Hobson 7.00

HORSE PLAYERS' WINNING GUIDES

_____BETTING HORSES TO WIN Les Conklin 10.00
_____ELIMINATE THE LOSERS Bob McKnight 5.00
_____HOW TO PICK WINNING HORSES Bob McKnight 5.00
_____HOW YOU CAN BEAT THE RACES Jack Kavanagh 5.00
_____MAKING MONEY AT THE RACES David Barr 10.00
_____PAYDAY AT THE RACES Les Conklin 7.00
_____SMART HANDICAPPING MADE EASY William Bauman 10.00
_____SUCCESS AT THE HARNESS RACES Barry Meadow 7.00

HUMOR

_____HOW TO FLATTEN YOUR TUSH Coach Marge Reardon 2.00
_____JOKE TELLER'S HANDBOOK Bob Orben 10.00
_____JOKES FOR ALL OCCASIONS Al Schock 10.00
_____2,000 NEW LAUGHS FOR SPEAKERS Bob Orben 7.00
_____2,400 JOKES TO BRIGHTEN YOUR SPEECHES Robert Orben 10.00
_____2,500 JOKES TO START'EM LAUGHING Bob Orben 10.00

HYPNOTISM

_____HOW YOU CAN BOWL BETTER USING SELF-HYPNOSIS Jack Heise 7.00
_____HYPNOSIS: WHAT IT IS, HOW TO USE IT Lewis R. Wolberg, M.D. 12.00
_____HYPNOSIS AND SELF-HYPNOSIS Bernard Hollander, M.D. 7.00
_____MODERN HYPNOSIS Lesley Kuhn & Salvatore Russo, Ph.D. 5.00
_____NEW CONCEPTS OF HYPNOSIS Bernard C. Gindes, M.D. 15.00

_____NEW SELF-HYPNOSIS Paul Adams 15.00
_____POST-HYPNOTIC INSTRUCTIONS—SUGGESTIONS FOR THERAPY Arnold Furst . 10.00
_____PRACTICAL GUIDE TO SELF-HYPNOSIS Melvin Powers 10.00
_____PRACTICAL HYPNOTISM Philip Magonet, M.D. 3.00
_____SELF-HYPNOSIS—A CONDITIONED-RESPONSE TECHNIQUE Laurence Sparks . . . 7.00
_____SELF-HYPNOSIS—ITS THEORY, TECHNIQUE & APPLICATION Melvin Powers 7.00
_____THERAPY THROUGH HYPNOSIS Edited by Raphael H. Rhodes 5.00

JUST FOR WOMEN

_____COSMOPOLITAN'S GUIDE TO MARVELOUS MEN Foreword by Helen Gurley Brown   3.00
_____COSMOPOLITAN'S HANG-UP HANDBOOK Foreword by Helen Gurley Brown 4.00
_____COSMOPOLITAN'S LOVE BOOK—A GUIDE TO ECSTASY IN BED 7.00
_____I AM A COMPLEAT WOMAN Doris Hagopian & Karen O'Connor Sweeney 3.00
_____JUST FOR WOMEN—A GUIDE TO THE FEMALE BODY Richard E. Sand M.D. 5.00
_____NEW APPROACHES TO SEX IN MARRIAGE John E. Eichenlaub, M.D. 3.00
_____SEXUALLY ADEQUATE FEMALE Frank S. Caprio, M.D. 3.00
_____SEXUALLY FULFILLED WOMAN Dr. Rachel Copelan 5.00

MARRIAGE, SEX & PARENTHOOD

_____ABILITY TO LOVE Dr. Allan Fromme 7.00
_____GUIDE TO SUCCESSFUL MARRIAGE Drs. Albert Ellis & Robert Harper 10.00
_____HOW TO RAISE AN EMOTIONALLY HEALTHY, HAPPY CHILD Albert Ellis, Ph.D. . . . 10.00
_____PARENT SURVIVAL TRAINING Marvin Silverman, Ed.D. & David Lustig, Ph.D. 15.00
_____SEXUALLY FULFILLED MAN Dr. Rachel Copelan 5.00
_____STAYING IN LOVE Dr. Norton F. Kristy 7.00

MELVIN POWERS MAIL ORDER LIBRARY

_____HOW TO GET RICH IN MAIL ORDER Melvin Powers 20.00
_____HOW TO SELF-PUBLISH YOUR BOOK Melvin Powers 20.00
_____HOW TO WRITE A GOOD ADVERTISEMENT Victor O. Schwab 20.00
_____MAIL ORDER MADE EASY J. Frank Brumbaugh 20.00
_____MAKING MONEY WITH CLASSIFIED ADS Melvin Powers 20.00

METAPHYSICS & NEW AGE

_____CONCENTRATION—A GUIDE TO MENTAL MASTERY Mouni Sadhu 15.00
_____EXTRA-TERRESTRIAL INTELLIGENCE—THE FIRST ENCOUNTER 6.00
_____HOW TO INTERPRET DREAMS, OMENS & FORTUNE TELLING SIGNS Gettings . . . 5.00
_____HOW TO UNDERSTAND YOUR DREAMS Geoffrey A. Dudley 7.00
_____MODERN NUMEROLOGY Morris C. Goodman 10.00
_____PALMISTRY MADE EASY Fred Gettings 7.00
_____PALMISTRY MADE PRACTICAL Elizabeth Daniels Squire 7.00
_____PROPHECY IN OUR TIME Martin Ebon 2.50
_____SUPERSTITION—ARE YOU SUPERSTITIOUS? Eric Maple 2.00
_____TAROT OF THE BOHEMIANS Papus 10.00
_____WAYS TO SELF-REALIZATION Mouni Sadhu 7.00
_____WITCHCRAFT, MAGIC & OCCULTISM—A FASCINATING HISTORY W.B. Crow 10.00
_____WITCHCRAFT—THE SIXTH SENSE Justine Glass 7.00

RECOVERY

_____DRAGON SLAYER WITH A HEAVY HEART Marcia Powers 12.00
_____KNIGHT IN RUSTY ARMOR Robert Fisher 7.00
_____KNIGHTS WITHOUT ARMOR (Hardcover edition) Aaron R. Kipnis, Ph.D. 10.00
_____PRINCESS WHO BELIEVED IN FAIRY TALES Marcia Grad 12.00
_____SECRET OF OVERCOMING VERBAL ABUSE Dr. Albert Ellis & Marcia Grad Powers . 12.00

SELF-HELP & INSPIRATIONAL

_____CHANGE YOUR VOICE, CHANGE YOUR LIFE Morton Cooper, Ph.D. 10.00
_____CHARISMA—HOW TO GET "THAT SPECIAL MAGIC" Marcia Grad 10.00
_____DAILY POWER FOR JOYFUL LIVING Dr. Donald Curtis 7.00
_____DRAGON SLAYER WITH A HEAVY HEART Marcia Powers 12.00

____DYNAMIC THINKING Melvin Powers 7.00
____GROW RICH WHILE YOU SLEEP Ben Sweetland 10.00
____GROW RICH WITH YOUR MILLION DOLLAR MIND Brian Adams 10.00
____GROWTH THROUGH REASON Albert Ellis, Ph.D. 10.00
____GUIDE TO PERSONAL HAPPINESS Albert Ellis, Ph.D. & Irving Becker, Ed.D. 12.00
____GUIDE TO RATIONAL LIVING Albert Ellis, Ph.D. & R. Harper, Ph.D. 15.00
____HANDWRITING ANALYSIS MADE EASY John Marley 10.00
____HANDWRITING TELLS Nadya Olyanova 10.00
____HOW TO ATTRACT GOOD LUCK A.H.Z. Carr 10.00
____HOW TO DEVELOP A WINNING PERSONALITY Martin Panzer 10.00
____HOW TO DEVELOP AN EXCEPTIONAL MEMORY Young & Gibson 10.00
____HOW TO LIVE WITH A NEUROTIC Albert Ellis, Ph.D. 10.00
____HOW TO SUCCEED Brian Adams 10.00
___I WILL Ben Sweetland 10.00
____KNIGHT IN RUSTY ARMOR Robert Fisher 7.00
____LAW OF SUCCESS Napoleon Hill (Two-Volume Set) 30.00
____MAGIC IN YOUR MIND U.S. Andersen 15.00
____MAGIC OF GETTING WHAT YOU WANT Dr. David J. Schwartz 15.00
____MAGIC OF THINKING SUCCESS Dr. David J. Schwartz 15.00
____MAGIC POWER OF YOUR MIND Walter M. Germain 10.00
____NEVER UNDERESTIMATE THE SELLING POWER OF A WOMAN Dottie Walters . . . 7.00
____PRINCESS WHO BELIEVED IN FAIRY TALES Marcia Grad 12.00
____PSYCHO-CYBERNETICS Maxwell Maltz, M.D. 15.00
____PSYCHOLOGY OF HANDWRITING Nadya Olyanova 10.00
____SALES CYBERNETICS Brian Adams 10.00
____SECRET OF OVERCOMING VERBAL ABUSE Dr. Albert Ellis & Marcia Grad Powers . 12.00
____SECRET OF SECRETS U.S. Andersen 10.00
____STOP COMMITTING VOICE SUICIDE Morton Cooper, Ph.D. 10.00
____SUCCESS CYBERNETICS U.S. Andersen 10.00
____THINK AND GROW RICH Napoleon Hill 12.00
____THINK LIKE A WINNER Walter Doyle Staples, Ph.D. 15.00
____THREE MAGIC WORDS U.S. Andersen 15.00
____TREASURY OF COMFORT Edited by Rabbi Sidney Greenberg 15.00
____TREASURY OF THE ART OF LIVING Edited by Rabbi Sidney Greenberg 10.00
____WINNING WITH YOUR VOICE Morton Cooper, Ph.D. 10.00
____YOUR SUBCONSCIOUS POWER Charles M. Simmons 7.00

SPORTS

____BILLIARDS—POCKET ● CAROM ● THREE CUSHION Clive Cottingham, Jr. 10.00
____COMPLETE GUIDE TO FISHING Vlad Evanoff 2.00
____HOW TO IMPROVE YOUR RACQUETBALL Lubarsky, Kaufman & Scagnetti 5.00
____HOW TO WIN AT POCKET BILLIARDS Edward D. Knuchell 10.00
____JOY OF WALKING Jack Scagnetti 3.00
____PSYCH YOURSELF TO BETTER TENNIS Dr. Walter A. Luszki 2.00
____RACQUETBALL FOR WOMEN Toni Hudson, Jack Scagnetti & Vince Rondone 3.00
____SECRET OF BOWLING STRIKES Dawson Taylor 5.00
____SOCCER—THE GAME & HOW TO PLAY IT Gary Rosenthal 7.00
____STARTING SOCCER Edward F Dolan, Jr. 5.00
____WEEKEND TENNIS—HOW TO HAVE FUN & WIN AT THE SAME TIME Bill Talbert . . 3.00

Available wherever books are sold or from the publisher.
Please add $2.00 shipping and handling for each book ordered.

Wilshire Book Company
9731 Variel Avenue
Chatsworth, California 91311

For our complete catalog, visit our Web site at:
www.mpowers.com